For Lucy

VIIIV

"The image is a dream. The beauty is real.
Can you see the difference?"

-*Illusions*, Richard Bach

JACK
ALEISTER

———

VIIIV

———

CHAPTER

I

THE BEGINNING OF THE END

I can feel the warmth of blood soaking my shirt as the breeze passes. The chill of this world's touch is a feeling I have missed since the beginning of this walk-through hell.

"You can't live without me Jack," they said, desperately gasping for air. "You will never survive."

They grip the ground to try to sit up, holding back the blood from pouring out into the gutter under the bridge. I bend down, reaching for the cig still burning on the ground. With a deep inhale of smoke, I look up at the sky and reminisce about my days chasing nightmares.

There is a wave of passion for this moment, as I feel to be at the end of the road. A cough of blood sprays my face, bringing my attention back down to the final death I hope to witness.

"You will be as you were. Just the sad, pathetic little kid you were always supposed to be," they said, using each deep breath to the fullest.

"You're right," I said, bringing the cig to my lips. "I will never be the monster you wanted me to be."

"Monster?! You were a god, Jack." They replied.

Taking in the last hit of the cigarette like it was my last breath, I drop the butt into the puddle of thick blood beneath my feet. With my eyes locked on theirs, I stand up to grab the gas can under the bridge, where it always was. I can feel false tears of sadness fill my eyes as they try to grab hold of me, knowing exactly what I have planned.

"You will cease to exist without me! Please... please don't do this!" They said, grabbing ahold of my leg to stop me from finishing this endless cycle. Without sympathy, I kick them off with an angry force and pop the cap of the jug of gasoline. The sound of distant sirens becomes loud enough that I believe they are coming to stop me, but this must happen. *Everything has led to this moment,* I thought, *I can't waste my opportunity.* Tilting the jug to spill, I drench their clothes in the pungent gas. The smell of blood and gasoline is a mixture I never thought I would sense, but I can feel my mind become victorious as it fills the air.

"You can never erase me," they said, watching me dig into my pocket and pull out my lighter. The one with the #85 engraved on the side of it. The same silver zippo that has been in my pocket since the beginning. They watch as I take pride in striking the flame and reach out, waiting for some kind of answer.

"I love you Jack." They said, taking in their final breath, knowing this was the end. I watch tears fill their eyes as I drop the lighter into the stream of gas and ignite the fire of my freedom. Feeling the flames grow higher and the warmth of relief, I softly reply.

"I know."

15 HOURS

As my story starts, I am just a regular kid. I have good grades, a job, and a great family with the best role models I could ever ask for, my parents. The town we live in has only about 10,000 people but always has someone new stopping through. Everyone wanted to see what the small city of "Pleasantville" had to offer, and they were never disappointed. The town had only the necessities, but the visitors had no interest in the sites, it was the overjoyed population. The happiness of the people. Everyone was a family of neighbors who loved each other. It was infectious for our guests as if it was a second chance for those who lived in darkness. That's why I loved my home. It was a haven.

My family always had a big part in the community and how things ran smoothly with my older brother Jacob, being the center point of most town meetings. People seemed to gravitate to his ideas and follow his lead with the young wisdom he offered. Even though he was only 18, he had plenty of accomplishments to be confident with the speeches he would occasionally deliver. He was the starting quarterback for Pleasant Highschool and the only contender for valedictorian this year. He's completed every race or challenge the town had to offer and won. He's been my hero ever since I've been able to stand on my own. The only person that could ever be equal to him would be my sister Jackie. She was the gifted one. Beautiful singing voice, perfect straight A's, and a personality that warms your heart. Always joyful and full of life. Her beauty only rivaled her charisma.

"Never settle for second best. Always fight for what's right. And never forget who loves you." she always said, reminding me each day.

But my parents are the real stars of the *show*. They were the inseparable and cliché high school sweethearts. Always finishing the other's sentences and always happy to be around each other. My dad was the hardworking and determined type of father. He wakes up early for work and stays up late to be with his family. Someone I could look to for help with questions of life and my homework. A true balance of his career and his home life. Being a loving husband and a great dad. That's why he made it a big deal to go fishing for the weekend. Just the boys, but not without Mom's famous turkey sandwiches. She made a point that I needed to eat more if I was going to grow up big and strong like my father. I always felt she loved me the most. I was like her baby that could never grow up, and she showed it, in public... Pinch your cheeks kind of mom. I would do anything for her. She is my best friend. I loved our relationship, and it was something I would never let go of.

Something I have always *wanted...*

ON THE NEXT EPISODE OF,
"THE PLEASANTVILLE FAMILY."

"TURN THAT FUCKING TV OFF AND GO TO BED!"
I am shaken awake by the sound of my mother.

"I'm havin' a friend over and I don't need him thinkin' I gotta BUM for a son!" my mother yells with a burning cigarette hanging off her lip. I feel her thick romance novel strike my chest as I rub my eyes, waking from my daydream.

"You think I was fuckin' kiddin' Jack?! GET UP!" she continued.

Stumbling down the hallway to my room, I hear a knock at the front door. *Must be one of her boyfriends,* I thought, as she rushed to open it. Putting on her mask of fake happiness.

"Coming!" she said with a smile on her face. An attitude I don't see anymore. Ever since my father was sent to prison for life. 1st-degree murder and several counts of domestic violence. Even though he is my father, he deserves it. I wish it would have just happened sooner before he had a chance to ruin this family, three years ago.

I reach my bedroom door as I hear the man come in, kissing Mother as she giggled. Feeling the cringe of the moment, I close my door and bury my head into my pillow. I lay there dreaming of my favorite TV show, thinking about what it feels like to have a family full of love and aspirations. To be held and told that you are loved. Having a smile on my face from the moment I wake up to the time I fall asleep. *Impossible.* I'm *just a kid from Chicago.* I thought, battling my dreams with reality.

With my mind on overdrive, fighting for a touch of happiness through imagination, I finally fall asleep.

TUESDAY 7:06 am

I wake up the next morning to the sound of my sister bursting through my door. I quickly open my eyes and see her collapse onto the floor, slamming her face into the carpet. As I sit up to see if she's ok, I get the sense that she is drugged out, once again, thinking this is her room. This is nothing new, but it gets harder each time she comes home like this. She has been this way ever since my father started selling crack to the neighborhood. She might as well have been his first customer. Everything seemed to be going right in her life before that happened. And now, I fear for her safety every day. It's as if she has given up on the world and the desire to live.

"Kim?" I said, hoping for an answer.

She begins to convulse with sounds of choking as I spring out of bed and rush to help her sit up. She's trying to throw up but has the vomit stuck in her throat, restricting her ability to breathe. It feels I have done this too many times now. Every time is unique, but it has never gotten any easier no matter how many times it happens. As I reach in to help her, I feel her body tense up.

"Get off me creep!" she slurs, swinging her arm back, almost striking me upside the head.

"Kim! It's Jack!" I said, trying to control her movements, waiting to block the next fist from coming my way. She lets out a roar of puke onto my pile of clothes I haven't folded yet. I close my eyes with disappointment from my lazy habits. *Fuck.*

"I said 'Get off me!'" She repeats as a second fist slips through my hands and lands square in my nose.

I am thrown back against my bed as she shuffles to her feet and stumbles back out of my room. Slightly dazed from the hit and still hazy from just waking up, I feel a single drop of blood hit my hand. I let out a deep sigh and stand up, gripping my nose. *I can't get blood on Mothers' carpet*, I thought, stepping into the hallway to get a tissue. On my way to the bathroom, I notice that my brother's door is cracked open. As I go by, I slow my pace to peek inside. He sits on the edge of his bed, building small dime bags of crack cocaine for his customers. There's a large amount of what I believe is baking soda with a small mound of rock cocaine. His strategy of cutting and selling the drug is courtesy of my father's knowledge. He taught him everything he knew. Even down to the hygiene within his room. It reeks of sour milk and body odor, with trash overflowing into the hallway like someone unloaded an entire dumpster through his window.

"What the fuck are you looking at Jack!" he yells as he looks up from his table. "Get the fuck out of here before I beat your ass again." He continued, now standing up with his fist clenched.

I don't even take a breath before running off into the bathroom and closing the door behind me. I hear him yell out while I try to catch my breath.

"Bitch!" he said before slamming his door.

I turn on the light and feel the brightness fry my eyes. Turning my vision a fuzzy darkness. As I blink to re-adjust my vision, I see myself in the mirror. My eyes open wide with shock when I see that the blood has reached my shirt. I realize I must have been dripping all over the apartment. My body begins to tremble with fear as I see that it's all over the sink at this point.

It's everywhere! I thought.

I quickly grab a tissue and begin to clean up in a panic, hoping Mother wouldn't find out I'm making a mess of her bathroom. As I look up from the sink, I catch a glimpse of my eyes in the mirror and feel a sharp flash of pain I know all too well.

"My headaches are getting worse," I said under my breath, knowing this to be a problem. But it seems my headaches have always been there. Like something I was born with. Something that will always be there, but I would never know why because Mother didn't believe in medicine, nor did she care enough about my health.

As I rub my eyes and take a deep breath, my pain smooths out to a bearable feeling. When I open my eyes, I see Mothers' 1990s alarm clock above the toilet.

"Ah fuck! I'm late!" I impulsively scream, most likely waking Mother up from her long night with her "friend."

I run back to my room in a fevered panic, grabbing my backpack and #2 pencil. I put on my hoodie, not even bothering to change my shirt and head back out. Trying to put my shoes on as I hop back through the hallway, my mother greets me like I knew I would. She looked at me with fire in her eyes. Visually upset that she was woken up so early. I stop and wait for the harsh words she most likely has for me. She stares deeply into my eyes quietly until I feel a swift slap to my face.

"I told you to be quiet in the mornings! I need my beauty sleep!" she yelled.

Even though she was my mother, there was nothing beautiful about her. Inside and out. She was a cold-hearted monster that could have been the star of a horror movie.

"And you're gonna be late for school again! I can't believe I have such a worthless loser for a son. You won't amount to anything in this world. How do you expect to pay the rent if you can't even wake up on time?" she said, cruelly stating the truth.

This is also nothing new but gets harder and harder to handle each time I go through this type of abuse. But it is getting to the point I'm starting to believe her. The cut on my nose reopens and starts to bleed again.

She doesn't even flinch, knowing it was probably her slap that drew blood. With tears in my eyes and a burning sensation from the hit, I continue towards the door, deciding to finish putting on my shoes outside.

Once I put on my other shoe and close the front door, I catch the sight of the late bus's taillights turning the corner. This would be the second time I was late this week, and it's only Tuesday. I obviously can't walk to school knowing it's 4 miles away and already late for my first period. I take off running hoping it gets stopped by a red light or some sort of traffic. I run as hard as I can but can't seem to close the gap. Luckily, I notice a train coming. I slow my pace as the bus comes to a complete stop. Out of breath, I run-up to the door and do my best to get the driver's attention. *I must look like a fool,* I thought. Jumping and waving my hands while still trying to regain my energy from chasing the bus. The driver finally acknowledges me and smiles. I calm down as I feel a sigh of relief from this morning. Reaching for the handle, I wait for him to open the doors.

"What's taking so long? Open the door man." I said myself as I looked back at the driver, wondering why he still hadn't opened the doors. But I find him just staring at me. Like he was stuck. I feel an uneasy breeze past as I watch his smile slowly bend and twist. My feeling grows with his pigmentation shifting to a pale white. The more I stare back at him, the more my stomach turns. Pulling on the door now, I struggle to understand what is happening.

Why is he fucking with me? I can't do this right now. I need to make it before I miss the entire first period and get an F for today, I thought. Trying to hide from the truth.

"Come on man, stop fucking around with me!" I shout as I look over and watch the last part of the train go by.

HONK! HONK!

"Hey kid, wake up! Are you getting in?" the bus driver said.

Looking back at the driver, I notice the doors are open, and everyone is just staring at me like I'm a crazy person.

"Hop in. We're going to be late," he said as I stood there in a daze. I step inside as he begins to question me.

"Are you ok kid? You seemed a little out of it there," he asked.

Reaching for the ceiling handrail, I continued to the back like I couldn't understand what he said. I try to shake it off and notice the bus is packed with staring eyes. All tracing me with judgment. I make it to an open seat to find why it's empty. It looks to be soaked in piss.

"Great." I said as I shook my head like I was not surprised.

"Kid! You're going to have to sit down, or you need to get off the bus. It's not safe, and I'm not about to lose my license because of you." the driver said over the speaker.

At that moment, I notice a young female wearing a hood stand up and head to the door. I quickly hurry over to her seat while my mind is still trying to process the last moments. As I slide past her, I get the smell of a hint of jasmine, just like Mothers' perfume. It was the one she always wore when everyone was happy.

Finally, I thought as I begin to relax in the window seat. While the bus driver picks up speed, I glance down to the sidewalk next to me. I see the girl in the hood that just got off and graced me with the seat. She seemed to be just a regular girl from the city: boots, dark jeans, and an oversized long jacket with the hood up. But I notice she is just standing there. It's as if she is looking directly at me, but I couldn't see her eyes. I feel a slight warmth of anxiety within my body as I lose sight of her.

"*NEXT STOP, SEVENTH AVENUE,*" the automated system states, followed by the bus chime. *BUZZZ*

I look down on my watch, knowing there is no way ill make it to first period, and instantly remember that my battery was dead. It completely slipped my mind last night to replace it. Enraged with anger and frustration, it feels I can't get a break, and personally, I don't make it any better. I am always so focused on my family and what my home life has become that it's hard to see the world.

I finally make it to school just in time for my first-period teacher to give me a write-up for being late once again.

"Thank you!" I said sarcastically with an energic tone as I walked out of the class.

"*Today is off to a wonderful start*!" I thought, knowing I am very much starting to be fed up with it.

Remembering what day it was, I begin to calm down, telling myself it will get better. Lying to myself that everything is going to be ok. *After all, it's Tuesday.* Tuesdays are always better.

TUESDAY

8:26 AM

Tuesdays are such an awkward day. It is not the "case of the Mondays," the joyful "hump day," or a "thirsty Thursday." Especially not everyone's favorites, Friday and Saturday. And it sure as hell was not a "Sunday Funday." It's boring ass Tuesday. It is just Tuesday. There is nothing special or extra about Tuesdays, but its placement in the week is perfect. It's like a day of recovery from a bad Monday, but not far enough in the week to be happy about it. But for me, it was my favorite day of the week because of my second period, Physics 2. Physics has always been my passion. Even before I knew people studied it. The idea that there are multiple dimensions and realities is just insane. That there are an uncountable number of alternate paths or decisions a singular person can make that can create a new universe. With 8 billion humans alive on this planet, it just blows my mind. That's why I take this class multiple times during the week. But on Tuesdays, Molly has Physics 2 also at 8:30 AM.

She was the prettiest girl in school. She was gorgeous, to be precise. Like something I have never seen before but see it every week. There was almost a shining light as I would notice her come into the classroom. And for that reason, I was always early. She was my north star in the dark world. Something that made me feel like it was all worth it, and there's hope to be happy once again. Unfortunately, I'm positive I am just a shadow in the room, even though we share the same desk. I was just the quiet, depressed kid in the black hoodie. Everyone already treated me that way, so it would be no surprise to come from the most popular girl in school.

This Tuesday was different though. Something felt off as I came around the corner to enter the class. She was early and set up for the period by the time I walked in. Stunned, I basically dance with anxiety in the doorway, doing my best to make a simple decision. Go in and sit next to her in the empty classroom, or run like I had forgotten something. Before I even get a chance to take my next breath, she brightens up as she sees me.

"Hey!" Molly said.

My mind twists with excitement and sadness. *There is no way she recognizes me. There's no way she would want to talk to me. There must be some mistake.* I thought to myself.

"Jack, right?" she asked.

Now it's my stomach. I feel as if the entire room starts to spin in every direction possible. I mutter what I can only describe as a foreign language.

"Eh..uh..yeah."

She isn't fazed, nor does she care that I am ghost-white with fear, and proceeds to ask me a question.

"I'm sorry to bug you with such a basic question. I should pay more attention in class and not on my phone, but I'm pretty sure there's a pop quiz today." Molly said with a slight flirting attitude.

Still standing in the doorway, I am gently pushed aside. It's my teacher, Mr. Cook. The same physics teacher that I have had for the past couple years.

"Standing there like a deer in the headlights isn't gonna pay the bills kid. Coming through!" Mr. Cook said as I'm knocked back into reality. I stumble forward as the rest of the class follows.

Completely oblivious of what just happened, I shuffle to my seat. I can barely get my stuff out and ready for the lesson before the late bell rings, louder than usual. *BUZZZ*

"Good morning class!" Mr. Cook said as he stood in front of his desk and addressed the students.

Struggling to find my #2 pencil, I finally spot it. It's

on the ground in the doorway where I did my record-breaking dance of nervousness.

"Jack," Molly whispered.

Sitting straight up in my seat with my eyes still wide, I remember the small interaction I just had with her. I proceed to stare at my unreachable fallen soldier of a pencil and act as if I couldn't hear her.

"Today is an easy day! Filled with fun and laughter and... a pop quiz!" Mr. cook said as he wiped the chalkboard clean. He was considered as some sort of comedian, or at least in his own eyes. As I try to refocus, I feel a hot pinch on the back of my arm.

"OWW!" I yelp as Mr. Cook turns around and acknowledges me.

"And there will be no 'lovey-dovey' time during this test." Mr. Cook said as the class softly chuckled and turned Molly and I bright red with embarrassment. He begins to hand out the test as I try to take in the last few moments of drowning in my mind.

"Easy and full of laughter like I said, so you guys should have no problem completing this test. I mean, unless you don't have a pencil! HAHAHA!" he said with a smile and laughed. Not me though. I'm still staring at my pencil, petrified with the start of my favorite class.

I glance at my watch as I remember it's still dead and look towards the clock hanging on the wall.

8:33 AM

"Are you kidding me?" I said under my breath. Realizing it has only been three minutes. Wishing I could run away and hide. Having the test now in front of me, I get lost in the first question.

"What does EMC squared stand for?"

It's as if Mr. Cook was fucking with me. *Did he really think people did not know this fundamental question in a physics 2 class?* Completely blown away, I get lost wondering why he would put this on a test. Then, a single yellow #2 pencil rolls across the desk onto the paper in front of me. I look over to Molly to notice she is looking straight back at me and gives me a wink. My motor skills seem to stutter as I reach for the pencil and drown inside.

WHAT THE FUCK IS GOING ON?

I start the quiz to take my mind off the overwhelming nervousness flowing through my body. The test is just as easy as the first question. I fly threw it and it takes me less than 10 minutes to complete. Having ample time to waste, I immediately return to my "deer in the headlights" look, staring at my pencil still in the doorway, replaying the start of the period. After a minute of focusing on this small inanimate object that has complete control of me, I began to drift. My imagination wanders as my mind begins to slip. I fall into a consciousness of being lost, and within just seconds, I feel a flash of peaceful darkness. I am no longer in Physics 2.

The smells of damp leaves and exotic plants are triggered in my mind. I can hear the running water of a small river nearby and the sound of birds in the trees above me. I can feel the heat from the sun, and it's so humid that I can taste it. My vision begins to clear, and I find myself in the middle of a dense jungle. My mind tries to make sense of the moment, but the beauty of the landscape captivates me. I am amazed by the sight of moss-covered trees draping over the jungles floor like a natural ceiling. Life is thriving everywhere I look. Realizing the tropical climate, I begin to sweat from the lack of wind. My body urges to move forward as I feel the ground beneath my feet. Moist and thick. I start to follow my urge and take a step, feeling the mud squish under my foot. Before I take a second step, it begins to rain. The water is warm. Like a nice shower, something I never thought possible given I have never left the city. Before I know it, I am walking at a cautious yet curious pace. Touching and seeing things I never thought I would see. Vines and branches hanging down to the ground with a river now in sight. Brimming with different fish and bugs everywhere. Flowers and plants of every color imaginable. Things I've only seen in books, but now was a reality.

After walking parallel to the river and inspecting every little thing for what felt like hours, I reach an opening in the trees. An almost perfect circle of grass and flowers, untouched by the over-crowding vegetation. As I get closer, I notice the river begins from a small body of fresh water in the center of the field. I continue to enter the opening towards the pond, enjoying the feeling of the sun on my face. I stop at the bank of the pond and kneel to drink. The ripples of the water calm, and I see my reflection as if it was a large hazy mirror. But there is something different about me. I look tired, run-down, and older. The look in my eyes is of someone who has given up. Instead of being anxious and shaken by the sight, I am calm and understanding. There is warmth and relief in my reflection's eyes.

My mind feels at peace but is suddenly changed to a feeling of being watched as I stand up from the pond. I glance towards the tree line across the field and see the silhouette of a hooded figure. Within the moment of realizing this, I hear something quickly moving from behind me. I spin around in a flare of panic, but it's too late. It's a massive animal, and I assume its intention is dire. It leaps before I can comprehend my next move and latches on to my leg, tackling me in the process. Its teeth sink deeper and deeper into my skin as I start to fall to the ground. I hear a whisper as I close my eyes from the pain, bracing for the hit.

"Jack."

I hit the ground hard and hear the eruption of laughter. When I open my eyes, I see nothing but bright fluorescent light above me. A hand reaches out and grabs ahold of mine. It's Molly, and she seems to be embarrassed as she speaks again.

"I didn't even hit you that hard Jack," she whispered.

"Ok, come on guys. Like I said, no messing around. This is a test, and I don't want to fail you because of this." Mr. Cook said as he looked up from his work.

I quickly get up off the floor and back into my seat, still dazed from my fall. *Was it all just a dream?* I thought to myself. *Was it all just my imagination?* I touch my leg and still can feel the beast's teeth sinking into the bone and the rush of adrenaline.

"Come on Jack. I didn't hit you that hard. You just weren't answering me like you were asleep with your eyes open." She whispered with guilt and frustration in her voice.

Still confused and wondering how long I was out of it, I look up at the clock.

8:50 AM

Have I only been sitting here for 5 minutes after finishing the test? It felt like hours of wandering inside that jungle. How could that be possible? How could this be real if everything I witnessed wasn't? I thought. As I start to question my reality, I look up at Molly. She is still looking straight back at me with question in her eyes.

What does she want? Why has she been so set on talking to me? What would I have to offer the prettiest girl in school? I thought, continuing to overthink and falling back into reality.

I notice a small piece of paper as she slides it across the desk. It reads.

"Do you know the answer to the first question?"

Of course. I thought with a mental sigh. It's my ability to be the biggest nerd in school and not that she has any interest in me or my life. What was once sadness and excitement when she first spoke to me became sadness with regret. I quickly write down the answer on the paper and ultimately do not see that Mr. Cook is still looking up at me, watching me. Studying me.

"Mr. Aleister! Stand up please." Mr. Cook said, triggering me into a survival mode.

"You really think I can't see you cheating this entire class? Every day is the same with you kids. You come in, can't be quiet, smelling of drugs and god knows what else, and now the A+ student proves he been cheating the whole time!" he said as I shook with fear and disappointment in myself. I try to speak, but it feels like my mouth has been wired shut. My mind races as I look for the words to plead my case but find nothing. I feel the student's eyes burning holes in the back of me as they chuckle and begin to whisper among themselves, judging me.

"It's Molly's fault!" I blurt out, trying to pull the words back into my mouth, but it's too late. She looks up at me with a burning anger. Following me with her eyes as she stood up.

"I didn't do anything Mr. Cook! This creepy nerd won't leave me alone. He keeps passing me answers to the test, trying to get me to sleep with him." She stated, defending herself in a gruesome stab to my heart. I am sick. A pain in my stomach so strong I feel myself drift towards blacking out. My eyes begin to swell with tears and heartbreak. *Of course, she wouldn't want anything from me other than use me and cast me away like a piece of trash.* But I never imagined that she would destroy my passion for her in front of the class.

"Mr. Aleister, go to the principal's office." Mr. Cook demanded.

The class quiets as they can feel the air sucked out of the room. All of them feeling my energy growing into a wave of colorful emotions. Stricken with embarrassment and anger, I gather my backpack and Molly's fake "nice gesture of a pencil." It burns in my hand like a glowing hot iron. I toss it on the desk and watch it roll over Molly's test. I am quick to turn back and get the hell out of there to hide and be away from this crippling moment. As I start for the door, I feel Molly begin to speak.

"Fucking creep." She said under her breath, but plenty loud enough for the class to become a small theater audience. I barely make it to the door as my vision begins to blur with a cloud of pain from one of my headaches. Swinging the door open, I make it out of the classroom and take a deep breath. It feels like the first breath I've taken since the bus ride here. With my vision still blurry, I make my way down the hallway, trying to focus on something to fight the pain. The student lockers line the walls, stretching the entire building. I figure they were the same ones from the opening of the school back in 1979. Beaten up and needing a new coat of paint since then. Each of them with its own personality. Stickers that peeled off poorly, bent in locks, and worse. Some are even missing doors completely. Those are usually given to the freshmen. I didn't use mine most of my first year. Everything getting stolen twice in the first week was money lost in my house. I didn't come to school for a few days after the second time. I was scared. Scared the teachers would see the bruises on my face. That was *before* my father went to prison.

"Stop! Think of something else!" I yell to myself.

I make it to the principal's office and knock gently, hoping it is not heard.

"Come in."

My face cringes when I hear the principal's voice from behind the door. I push my way in and stand inside the office, but my mind is not there. I can't see or hear anything. I'm in a daze, trying to think of anything other than my mom and what she will do to me when she finds out. She was already bothered with me for being late and now this. *She is going to kill me.* I thought as he slid a paper across his desk that read.

SUSPENSION NOTICE

Dear Mrs. Aleister,

Your son was in a sexual harassment incident with a student today. We take specific measures to ensure our student's safety and this type of conduct is unacceptable. As the principal of this school, I have no choice but to take disciplinary actions. Jack is to stay home from school for the next three days and can return to his regular schedule this coming Monday.

Principal Collins

I knew it was coming, but I had hope. Hope that it wouldn't have been a suspension. Hope that was wasted. Something I have little to let go of freely. The late bell snaps me out of it, and I reach for the notice, grabbing it like it's going to bite me. I slump out into the hallway filled with students and just stand there, drained of what little energy I had. For a moment, I look for an opening to what I can only describe as fish swimming upstream. It feels as if I bump into every kid on my way to the front door. One step at a time, I make my way back through the physics area and see Molly. She is laughing and having a *great day.*

"Bitch." I said, still moving through the swarm of students and reliving the moment just a few minutes ago.

I am almost to the door when I get a slight whiff of jasmine. My mind flashes to the girl I saw on the bus as

I see the same jacket pass me through the crowd. Before I realize this, I am shoved outside by what I'm guessing was the school bully. I hit the ground and cement my feelings for the start of this day. *Fuck man, can it get any worse?* I thought. As the sun touches my skin, I feel a burning sensation and my headache becomes a sharp blade in my mind. The feeling passed as quickly as it came, returning a small amount of energy. I stand up and let out a sigh of grief.

"I guess I'll head close to work," I said, trying to shake off the physical pain.

WORK

After sitting on the bench across the street from my job for hours, you would think I would have done something more with my time. At least gotten something to eat. But the only thing that was on my mind was Molly. How she extinguished any sort of light I had in my life. My north star. To see her and dream of just conversations with her. Just to be in the friend zone would have been good enough for me.

"Fucking creep" keeps ringing in my head like a favorite song. It's enough to make anyone sick.

I made sure to be an hour early to work, given I've been outside for hours. Honestly, I really needed this. To be focused on something so mindless and tedious. I was the cook's assistant at the local college pizza spot. It was called "*Something Pizza.*" It was a small hole-in-the-wall place with a neon sign, wooden seating, and big front windows. Traditional décor you would see in most older pizza places. We sold beer and basic pizzas for cheap. So the college kids loved it. Great place to mess around with your friends and talk to singles. There was always something going on. But of course, Tuesdays were our busiest nights. 2$ slices with 2$ draft beer. I may be 17, but the owner Jim didn't care about me serving underage. All he cared about was the money and how much was being made. He always said before every shift.

"Don't serve the cops! And if you serve a narc, you're fired!"

He was an older man that has probably seen his fair share of troubled times. I always figured he knew *what* was wrong but could care less. He only cared about who was paying him and when. I always liked him because he gave me the opportunity, but he was always an asshole. Yelling at me for his own faults and forgetting with his old age. He had a loveable *"Get off my lawn you kids!"* kind of vibe, and I couldn't help but enjoy that about him.

It gets to the last 30 minutes of my shift, and everything has gone great. I had almost completely forgotten about what happened earlier. Still trying to let go of what will happen when Mother finds out that I've been suspended. Then I see a couple come through the side door and head to the server's desk. By no surprise of how my day has turned out, I notice the female. It's Molly, and she is with the high school Jock named Jeff. My body feels like it sinks through the floor, remembering what happened today. *This was supposed to be my escape from everything. From everyone.* I thought. My mindless job. A place I was able to forget. My last defense in this world I live in. But now she stands there, waiting to be ushered to a table with her date. I check my watch to see if it was late enough to leave but forget the battery is still dead. I walk up to the front and place my hands on the counter. My body tenses and freezes over with shame. I feel as if the "deer in the headlights" has just been struck by a semi-truck. She looks away from Jeff, still giggling like she is in love and catches eye contact with me.

"We'd like a table for two, please. Preferably next to the window." She said, still giggling from *Mr. Right's* joke.

Does she not know who I am? I question myself as my head begins to hum with pain. *How does she not see that she completely ruined my life just hours ago?* I stand there, dazing off into her eyes unwarranted. Still unable to move.

"Hey bro, can he get the table or what?" Jeff asked.

"Yes! Ah sorry! Right this way!" I take them to the best table in the place and seat them.

"I think we are going to start with a couple of beers," Jeff said as he pulled the seat out for Molly. "And two waters please." Molly continued.

"You got it," I replied, turning around and cowering inside my shell of emotions like a turtle. As I walk back into the kitchen, I hear Jim yell for me over the crowd and ring the bell.   BUZZZ

"Order up! Two slices of pep!"

I rush over to the slices and serve the guys in the back as I glance at the clock.

9:48 PM

Knowing my shift is done in just a few minutes, I see my co worker come through the kitchen. I quickly grab my replacement with relief and bring him to Molly's table. We walk up immediately and interject without hesitation. *I need to get out of here.*

"Hi. I am closing out. This is Ken, and he will be taking over the rest of your order."

Molly and her date stop their conversation as if I'm causing a train wreck in the heart of downtown. They both look up at me with disapproval, something I am already too fond of.

"Ok yeah, whatever," Molly said as she takes a double look at me, "Wait, aren't you the guy in my class? Jack, right?"

Holding back the pain I have dealt with for the last couple of hours, I respond.

"Uh..Yeah, that's me." I shrugged with an uneasy smile.

With my response, Jeff is now interested and sits straight in his seat, looking me up and down.

"This is the guy?" he asked as he glanced back at Molly. "This is the guy that I heard about sexually harassing you?"

Feeling as I did in class, I quickly speed the conversation up and hope it rolls over like nothing ever happened.

"Uhh.." I stutter, trying to put together words but quickly cut off.

"You're the guy that's been hitting on my girlfriend," Jeff said as he stood up out of his seat, clinching the table like it was a piece of paper. Watching as his "alpha," uneducated, male mind instinct turn on. Ready to beat my ass for something I never did. *How could I harass her without even speaking to her, let alone look in her direction?* I turn around to go back to the kitchen when I feel his hand grab hold of my arm.

"I'm not done talking to you nerd." He shouted with a different look in his eyes.

He spins me back around to face the table. The situation has become so awkward that the guy covering my shift, Ken, has left me there to be eaten by the wolves. I look at Molly and she seems to be unshaken by the moment. Just completely fine with the idea of her date beating me to a pulp for something she lied about. I began to sweat with panic and frustration. I feel a slight tickle of pain in my head as I see a yellow #2 pencil roll across the table towards me.

"I'm gonna teach you a real lesson you can't get from any book creep!" Jeff said, reaching back to give me a punch to the gut. The slight tickle of pain in my head turns to a heated flare of agony. My vision burns black as I feel my hand reach out and quickly snatch the pencil off the table. Without a second to understand my body's movements, I begin to thrust the #2 pencil into his neck with precision. Jeff's eyes look upon me with dread and panic. Before I can blink, I find myself piercing his skin, deep, just under his jawline. His blood begins to gush and spray over me like a warm shower. As I take my first breath since this all started, I notice a cigarette being lit just outside the window across from the table.

"What's going on over here? I will have no fighting in my restaurant," Jim calmly said as he walked up to the table. My eyes flicker as I notice I have not moved an inch.

"This place fucking sucks anyways old man! Let's go Molly." Jeff said, letting go of my arm and reaching for Molly's hand.

Shaking my head to snap back into reality, I step out of the way of the girl who broke my heart. As she walks away, I feel as if any light that could be left inside is dragged away like roadkill under someone's car. Confused and worried about myself, I walk back to the kitchen to finally clock out and get ready to take on the next difficult part of this *shit* day. Home. I grab my bag and my slice of pizza I always get after a shift when Jim stops me.

"Look Jack, I really don't want to do this, but I can't have you messing up the money flow and that order just cost me 23 dollars." He explained with a face I didn't want to see after my confrontation.

"I'm gonna have to let you go. I can't afford mistakes like that," he said, handing me what I can only assume is my last check.

BUZZ BUZZ

I feel my phone vibrate in my pocket. Given I am in no way a popular person, I quickly pull it out with curiosity and the need to hide from the moment. Without reading, I notice it's a notification from *YouTube,* and the video starts.

Creep gets called out in class.
CRINGE WARNING

I open the app to find that it is a video from one of my classmates. My heartbreaking moment with Molly today in its entirety for the world to see. Not only did the 13 other students witness my destruction, but there were also more than 50,000 views. Comments. Likes. Shares. I have become a viral laughingstock in mere hours. Tears fill my eyes, trying to fight the darkness that is swallowing me whole. My body begins to tremble with anger and destitute. I feel my mind, body, and soul give up all at once. I look up from my phone with glazed-over eyes, looking into the depths of Jim's soul as he continues.

"I'm sorry."

MAKE A WISH

Is this really what it feels like to lose everything? To feel as if you would be better off dead? Who would really care? My mother? Father? My brother and sister? No one would be affected if I just didn't come home one day. If I just ceased to exist. No one would be any different. *Is this what It feels like to have given up?* To have finally let go of any love I have for myself.

"Do I even dare to go home?" I ask myself, walking out of the pizza place and onto the street.

"There's no way I can tell her. She is just going to hit me again. Over and over until I run and hide in my room." I said, stepping out to the damp sidewalk.

With tears in my eyes, I start my journey home. I

usually take the bus after work on Tuesday nights, but I didn't want to even try. I didn't even want to walk, but my feet kept taking step after step like an organic pacemaker, keeping my heart from stopping.

The night was cold and wet. It must have rained while I was at work. The sides of the buildings soaked, with the potholes in the street, full. The smell of water saturates the air as I take a deep breath to focus on anything but my day. I see the bus pass me as I cross the street into the darker area of the city. The part that doesn't get too many visitors because of its crime rate. I have done the walk more times than I can count, but I always was cautious. Tonight was different. It was like I was looking for a reason to die.

Maybe I would be missed if my death were tragic. Maybe I would be missed if it wasn't my fault.

I turn the corner down an alley, wall to wall with trash and any furniture type you can think of. Mattresses, broken chairs, shattered glass everywhere, and trash bags stacked taller than my brother. It is something you would expect from this neighborhood, even with the smell of piss and rotting meat.

"I've never walked this route," I said to myself, moving past a drunk bum lying next to one of the stained mattresses.

"What?" he slurred, shaking his empty bottle of whiskey half asleep.

I do my best to continue through the alley, but I can't move any faster with my thoughts acting as a ball n chain strapped to my ankle. The deeper I walk through the city, the more I hear fights and sirens. An authentic soundtrack to this place. It is the ghettos voice. Always crying out for help. A harmony of pain. Something that's always been. I can almost guess how many different gunshots I hear on my late nights doing homework.

"Make a wish." Asked a small voice from within the dark.

My feet stop like I've stepped onto a patch of quicksand, slowly sinking into the earth. I turn in the direction of a voice and see a single burning cigarette. I get the weird sense they have been waiting for me to come down this way. Anticipating my arrival. They confidently step closer, and I see the cig burn a bright red. Inhaling deep, they come into the dimming lights of the alley. It was a female, slim and somewhat short. She was wearing a long jacket with the hood up and jeans.

Wait-. I thought, stopping my river of thoughts like a wall of silence. *Is that the girl from the bus?* I question, watching my sanity slip, and I get a slight hint of jasmine through the damp breeze. My entire body buzzes like I feel every nerve. I drift back a step and again question myself.

Is she following me? I swear she was everywhere I was today. She couldn't be following me. This is just blind luck.

She steps in front of me and pauses. I can feel her eyes watching me, but I still can't see her face.

"11:11... You're supposed to make a wish." She said softly, stopping close enough to touch.

She reaches up with her cigarette, still burning in her left hand, and pulls down her hood. Long black hair spills out and caresses her body. Her smile lights up her blue eyes like a full moon over the ocean. Her skin is smooth as her confidence, and her warmth is just as powerful. She tilts her head waiting for my response as I get lost in her beauty.

"Uh..yeah." I said quickly, regretting opening my mouth and looking down at my watch to check the time, and it *reads*.

11:11 PM

"Oh right. I knew that." I said, looking back up at her wishing I didn't.

"Well? Aren't you going to make one?" she replied, waiting patiently for my wish.

Troubled by the moment, I fall into the depths of my mind searching for an easy answer to such a difficult question. I find nothing but darkness and hate. Any light that was left in my life was snuffed out in the last 15 hours. I had nothing to wish for. Nothing could ever put together my family, give myself friends, or even have a girl crush on me. So why would I even give myself the hope of it being real? Why would I hurt myself again after all this?

"I wish I were dead," I replied with a clone of her confidence.

"Don't say that. Today is a great day! After all, it's

my favorite day of the week. It's Tuesday!" She replied, drowning me in her blue eyes.

I hesitate with her enthusiasm and joyfulness blocking me from moving like a prisoner. It is like she is untouched by this world. From its dark places and bad memories. She was full of life and happiness. Like an angel. *But what was she doing down here in the gutters of the city? She must have been following me. Why else would she be in this dark and depressing place only drug users and criminals call home?*

"It's really not all that bad. Trust me." She said, trying to keep my interest. "Life is full of happiness. You just need to open your eyes to find it."

But what is happiness if you have never felt it? How do you know when you have found it and live with it? What is happiness? Is it success? Health? Wealth? Love? Or is it just acceptance?

"Ok fine. I just wish I could get a retry for today." I said, feeling her optimism become contagious.

She continues with beautiful words and cheerful looks as I dive deeper and deeper into her eyes while she talks. Filling my heart with every sound coming from her lips and perfect smile. I can't help but drift off, dreaming about her when I snap back into the moment, pulled by a force I cannot describe.

"So, where are you going? Home?" she asked softly, expecting a response.

"Yeah. I'm going hom-." I pause, not wanting to finish my answer.

She puts on her best pouty face like she understands my pain. She begins to tell me about herself and how she doesn't have a home. She expresses the tragedy and sorrows of her life like a quiet lone wolf crying for the moon. Soft and gentle with such difficult memories. I feel the connection between us grows as the pain we share makes us in common. It is something I never thought a pretty girl like her would go through. But she kept a positive outlook on it all like she was a professional with depression. I can't help but just stare at her, listening to every word she said like it was a small gift to me.

"You're going that way, right? We can walk together!" She said, lifting her hand from her side as if she wanted to hold my hand.

"Come. Walk with me in hell." She giggled, taking hold of my hand.

The feeling of her hand is freeing like a release of tension built up over the years. Her skin is as soft as I imagined, like silk through my fingertips with a gentle grip. She turns to head down the alley, pulling me wherever she wants. Walking through the alley and up the street, she continues to bless my ears with her words of inspiration and victory through hard times. She even has a fun little attitude about it with quick jokes and humor. We walked for 30 minutes, talking about our lives and how she had overcome it all until we stop at my street. I am lost. Not my location in the city but in a trance of wonder and disbelief. As we stop, I take a second and try to understand the events of the day. How I ended up holding hands and having a deep, meaningful conversation with the girl of my dreams. *How did this happen? Where did she come from? Is this why she was following me?*

She turns in front of me with the same smile she greeted me with, her blue eyes set on mine. She takes in a small deep breath and reaches her arms around me. I feel her warmth of the embrace and melt into her arms like we are two puzzle pieces finally connecting. I feel my body surge with passion and hope that seconds turn into hours holding her. I want to live in this moment forever. With her. I am happy for just a moment until I feel the slight chill from the breeze and a *puncture* to the back of my neck. My vision fades to black before thinking of anything more than her.

"I love you Jack."

"When we enjoy life, we see nothing. But when we hate life, we see everything."
-Jameson Aleister

THE BASEMENT

When I wake, I just lay there like a hangover just hit me like a truck. Feeling cold, wet concrete on my face with the smell of cigarettes and dust. It's dark, but I can see the walls are made of brick and a narrow wooden staircase directly in front of me. My body feels like it is about to give up with my energy continuing to decline. I try to move my legs to stand and notice a chain wrapped around my ankle like a snake. Gripping tighter and tighter the more I struggle. My panic sets in like a rogue wave, waking me from a drugged state.

"Wait, what's going on?" I ask myself, feeling a drop of sweat come down my nose.

"How did I get here?... Is this a basement?" I say

under my breath. As I try to sit up, I realize I also have a nice set of handcuffs, a police issue.

"Holy fuck! This is a basement. I'm in somebody's basement!" I scream.

Now fully aware of the situation and now sweating through my shirt, I remember that girl I met in the alley. The one with the hood up and smelled of jasmine. I remember how beautiful she was with the deepest blue eyes and a personality that was so soft with a rock-hard defense. How we walked home together and how she made me feel like I wasn't alone in this world. That there was a way out, and I felt it was with her. She was perfect. Like something out of one of my dreams. Like I created her out of thin air in one of my darkest moments. But what I don't remember is anything after we got to my street or how I got here.

"Hi there sleepy head." Said a voice I recognized from the corner of the room. I look over to see the spark of a match being lit to a cigarette. Knowing exactly who is standing there, I ask her what is happening. Hoping she would tell me that it's all a prank. That there was some misunderstanding. *A prank that you do to random people at night?* The thought crosses my head as I doubt my own idea of hope. Hearing her boots step forward before I can see her, she exhales, adding more smoke to the thick clouded room. I brace myself like I have a natural defense against predators.

"So. I'm sorry that you're all chained up and stuff, but I didn't want to scare you away." She cautiously stated.

"You could have run off and maybe gotten killed." She finished, stopping entirely in the light of the single hanging lamp.

"Killed?" I said.

"Well, yeah," she said, looking at me with a lush gaze. "I want to protect you. You're everything to me." she continued, putting me into an overwhelming discomfort.

How could she say that? I only just met her then she drugged me and chained me to a post in a basement. Is she crazy? Is she a serial killer waiting to make me cry as she slits my throat? Her smile grows as she drops the cig and steps it out with the heel of her boot.

"I'm your wife Jack. You don't recognize me?" she said, bending down to get closer.

Yeah, she is definitely crazy. I thought, squishing my back into the post as she leans closer. I burst out in words with no second thought.

"How could you be my wife? I just met you." I yelled. "And why would my wife kidnap me? Why would she scare me half to death just to protect me?"

She feels my tone of a frightened animal and gives me her pouty face. It's the exact look as the first time I saw it. Adorable and hard to be afraid of someone looking so trustworthy. But it's like her facial expressions are programmed. To be perfect every single time.

"I knew you would say that." She giggled like she was ready to read my next line. "I know everything about you Jack," she said, throwing my mind into a spiral of the unknown.

"You're my world, and I would do anything for you. I love you." She expressed with tears of love in her eyes. "You're the whole reason I'm here."

I begin to search in my mind for an answer to all this. Looking for any reason that this could be a dream. How this could be happening to me. If this was somehow true. *But how could it?* While I try to focus, I start to slide up the pole trying to stand, watching her stand with me. Looking down into her eyes, I get lost again. Searching for any way this could be true. *How would she know my name if she was just some crazy person?* I fight with myself as I begin to believe her. She has a hold of my thoughts like an unbreakable, gentle embrace. I am truly her prisoner.

"Just trust me, ok Jack?" she said, grabbing my hand and showing the diamond ring on her left hand.

"We will be home soon." she smiled, looking back at the neon clock on the shelf.

3:11 AM

She continues to watch me, now touching my handcuffs and grabbing something from her pocket. She pulls out a key and unlocks my restraints, looking for any trust I may have in believing her. I am torn between what I am told is my life and the life I live. *Would it be so bad if I believed her? What would I have to lose? I already have nothing to live for?* I ask myself, rubbing the handcuffs off my wrists. *What's the worst that could happen?* I don't hesitate to breathe easier, knowing anything would be better than going home. She then takes off the chain around my leg and stands up closer than before. Her beauty is almost blinding as my eyes grow to see it all. She pulls me in close and shows me what it feels like to be loved with a soft kiss on my lips. I push into her lips as my thoughts fly above the sky like I was looking down on myself within the moment. Her lips heal my pain and confusion with just one kiss. Everything washed away like a sandcastle on the shore. All the pain I felt at home with abusive parents and neglective siblings. The issues I've always had making a social life bearable for myself. And the lack of hope for someone to ever love me. All of it. Gone for just a moment until I'm pulled back, looking back at her with true love in her eyes.

"Let's go. We can't be late." She said grabbing me by the hand. Pulling me to follow, we head towards the wooden stairs in the center of the cold basement.

"Where are you taking me?" I asked.

"To the place we first met." She replied with a wink.

We make it up into the house and I realize it seems familiar. I'm hesitant, but I don't pay too much attention to the detail as my mind is set on watching her. Mesmerized by her gaze looking back at me every other couple steps like my hand clinched with hers wasn't enough. I feel the chill of the night as we step out onto the street. It's late enough to have the streets emptied but not early enough for the warmth of the sun. The stars shine in the scenery of her, guiding us in a direction only she knows. I look down at my watch and it *reads*.

3:33 AM

"Just over the hill and under the bridge." She said, pointing with her free hand. "We are almost home."

Why is she taking me here? I wonder as we walk over the hill and see the bridge just a few steps away. We stop just before the underpass when she speaks with enthusiasm.

"Ok, we are a little early, but this is it. Are you ready?"

THE END OF THE
BEGINNING

We stand there just staring up at the moon and still holding hands. Trying to soak up every second of the time we shared. I can feel myself shake with a nervous twitch, waiting for an answer from this mysterious girl when I'm shocked with the realization that I still don't know her name. *How have I been so busy with what is going on that I never asked for her name?* She turns from watching the moon and looks up into my eyes like she heard my thoughts. I hesitate with disappointment as my lips quiver, getting ready to ask her.

"You already know Jack. You're the one who created me," she whispered, placing one finger across my lips.

Stunned by the confidence in her voice, I let go of her hand, scared. Another twist in the plot like a writer had no idea what to do with her character. I begin to try to talk again to ask what she meant by created when she stops me with more words of a thousand questions.

"Shhh...he's almost here."

With every hair on my body standing straight up, I finally get to speak. I let out my words as if they are fired from a gun. Quick and loud to get attention.

"Who's coming?!" I scream. "Why are you being so secretive? What do you mean I created you?" I demanded, now upset with confusion and anxiety.

"Who are you?"

As she perks up and gives me the big smile I fell in love with, she pushes me back and steps away under the bridge. Lighting another cigarette, still staring at me with her deep blue eyes.

I hear quick footsteps behind me, growing in speed and volume as they get closer. I feel the rush of wind as I see a shadowed figure pass me. Wearing a long-hooded jacket, with boots. I can see the shine of a weapon in their hands but can't make it out with constant flickers of confusion.

"Run Jack!" a male voice calls out with concern in his voice.

Without hesitation, he takes his final step and drives

a katana into her chest, piercing her heart. I feel her blood hit me like a sneeze. Everything goes silent as I watch in disbelief and feel my mind shatter into a million pieces. It's as if my vision was a movie on tv and the screen cracked open. She lets out a gentle sigh of relief as she falls to the ground. Still staring at me, smiling.

"I love you Jack. You were always my favorite." She said, blood now seeping out of her mouth, staining her teeth a dark red.

"I'll see you at home. Go," she said with a loving and caring voice, trying to hold on to the moment she got to spend with me.

"WHAT THE FUCK ARE YOU DOING KID. RUN JACK!" the man yells, thrusting the blade deeper into the kidnapper I fell in love with.

Swallowed by heartbreak and fear, I feel my legs move as if I wasn't in control. One after another, I take steps back, not breaking eye contact with her. *How can this be happening? Why does this have to happen*? Even it was just for the better half of an hour, I've never felt so whole. She really did love me. She really did care for me. I could feel it. *But how is this possible?*

I make it to the corner, but I can't leave her like that. Even if it seems it was what she wanted. Even if she seemed crazy and was feeding me a lie. She was a human being and I can't let this guy just get away with this. But I couldn't stand up to him. I'm just a skinny 17-year-old boy. How could I defend her against a sword-wielding adult man? Anyone for that matter. I pull out my phone and dial 911. It's almost instantaneous that I get a response. The operator says they're sending someone out when I look back up at the murderous scene of my newfound love. Looking through the fence, wishing I could do something to save her. I watch as he pulls the sword from her chest with her no longer staring at me. I can see her say something to the man as he bends down and grabs her cigarette, inhaling deeply. He stands with a few gestures and grabs a gas can sitting inside the underpass. Sirens sound in the distance as he starts to pour gas on her bleeding body while she grasps for air. It feels I am watching my own horror movie as he sparks his lighter. With complete control, he drops it into the puddle of fresh gasoline. Igniting her body in a roaring fireball.

"Noo!!" I scream as my only chance at love is ripped from my eyes.

The man quickly looks back, not realizing he is being watched and starts to head in my direction with intent. Gripping his katana like I was next. I turn and run as hard as I can in the only direction I know, my bed. With the tears of pain fueling each step, I don't even look to see if he is following me. I just keep running. The further away I got, the more I needed to be free from my thoughts. I finally see an open window to the local grocery store and use my last steps of energy. I reach the window and begin to pry at it, hoping to get shelter from the killer. Completely out of breath and strength, I feel my mind fall out of my head, completely out of oxygen.

My vision goes black as I climb in and collapse onto the grocery store floor.

AISLE 9

As I wake up, still hazy from the fall, I just stare up at the ceiling. Unaware of my last moments. I notice an interesting burn mark directly above me but have little time to understand it when I hear footsteps. All at once, my mind shakes with the memories of the girl and her killer. I push myself to sit up but only can move at a snail's pace. I look down the aisle from where I can hear someone coming and wait for them to reveal their face. The closer the footsteps get, the more my body begins to hum with fear. A hooded figure wraps the corner, and my fear is reinforced. Within what felt like a second, he approaches me with a cautious pace. For some reason, he has a worried look on his face. He slowed to a stop in front of me and bent down. My nerves fire and I slide back like a traumatized dog. Terrified with the memories of the night flashing into my vision. I am forced by my emotions to scream out.

"You could have taken anyone! Anyone in this world! Why did you have to take her? Why!?" I cry out, demanding to be answered.

He takes down his hood and I recognize his face. Cold and tired, like he had given up. But I see warmth and relief in his eyes as he sees I am uninjured. I feel like I've seen him before but can't think of who. He resembles someone that could be my brother but 15 years older than me. Same brown hair that I have, same blue eyes, and the same facial hair my father would have.

He looks at me with deep compassion and love as his eyes fill with tears.

"I'm sorry Jack, but it had to be done." He said, now sobbing like he never wanted to do such a murderous thing.

"Why did it have to be her?! She was the only one who understood me. Someone who actually wanted to hear me speak. A person that loved me!" I weep.

"I know," he said, pausing briefly like it was hard to speak to me. "I was told it would never be easy, but it always had to be done. Every time." He continued, holding back the tears.

Searching for an answer, I find some understanding from it all. I try to shake it off like a fly on my food, but I am pulled deeper as he continues to speak.

"We've been here *84 times* in this very spot." He said, looking up at the burn mark on the ceiling above me.

"*But you're different Jack. You're 85.*" He continued, unclipping his necklace and holding it out for me to grab.

Flustered with confusion, I feel my soul pulsate out of my body. I stand up and try to think of a response to such a mentally draining statement. I feel as if I am connected with him in every word he speaks. As I grab the necklace with the intent of needing answers, it hits me like a ton of bricks.

"I don't understand," I said, finally realizing who he reminds me of. The exact reflection I saw from my dream in the jungle pond. Me. The same person, just older.

"The necklace will help you see." He stated, gesturing for me to put it on.

Without hesitation, I clip on the necklace and feel a surge of energy flow through my body. The power from the necklace is so intense that my body gives out. I watch as a single beam of light emits from the pendent. Shooting directly through the burnt spot in the ceiling. As I question this, my vision goes black, and my consciousness drifts.

"Good luck Jack. We're counting on you."

BETWEEN THE CRACKS

I am nothing but thought. Just the feeling of simplicity and dullness. I don't feel that I am connected to anything. A bodyless mind drifting without pain or uncertainty.

What is this? Where am I? Am I dead? I am calm. Like a cool breeze. Like a Tuesday.

As I fall deep into the abyss of existence, I see nothing but a tiny dot in the center of my vision, growing larger. I feel myself moving at a running pace towards it. The closer I get, the more I understand where the light is coming from. I am stopped promptly, floating above what seems to be three rooms with no ceiling. As I try to understand what I am looking down into, I notice someone come into the first room. My bones vibrate like guitar strings when I realize that it's me. He stops dead center of the room and stares into my eyes with a cold expression. I feel the air ripped from my lungs as I try to comprehend what I am witnessing. My vision distorts as my consciousness is pulled from the inside out. Watching as my body descends beneath me. My body turns and looks up at me with questioning eyes and asks,

"Why?"

I feel I can answer the question without hesitation, but I turn around to see what's behind me. My eyes fold with theories and ideas as my mind melts with confusion. I can see multiple versions of myself floating above me in a line, each one above the other. They're all dressed differently but move together in sync. The only thing I can do is ask.

"Why?"

My vision shifts again as my mind is forced through itself above me, into this other *me*. I watch as I am transported into different versions of myself. Over and over. Faster and faster. Each version showing me its own past and present memories in an instant. Every one of them including a memory of the girl with the hood. Each with a different traumatic event involving the loss of her. I begin to understand as my brain starts to fry from the continuous strain on my mental state. It becomes too much to handle and just before I pass out, I am slowed.

I see one last version. Long black jacket with the hood up, blue jeans and hi-tops. He looks exactly like what I believe to be the real me. But who is the real me?

I stop just in front of myself. Floating there in emptiness. He reaches out for me and places a lighter in my hand with confidence. I look down and see that it's a silver zippo with Roman numerals engraved on its side. "*VIIIV.*" *Eight-five,* I thought. I open the top and spark the flame watching the "real" version of myself smile with joy and victory. I am drawn to stare into the flame as it grows bigger and brighter. The space around me glows red with warmth. Before I can understand why, I see only red and feel my mind go dark.

ROOM 404

I wake up on the floor of a hallway. Feeling the carpet on my cheek and the flow of air conditioning. My eyes open to the sight of chandeliers hanging from the ceiling. I stand to my feet to see the décor is of a high-end hotel, lined with rooms and a few service carts. I try to remember the last few moments of how I got here and can't reason why nothing is clear. I move down the hallway at a slow pace in search of answers or clues on why I was here. As I walk by the first two doors, I can hear music that I recognize. One of my favorite songs. I think the title was "Paradise." It gives me a relaxing feeling as I pass the third door. It cracks open just slightly as I stop. I have the sudden urge to peek inside but tell myself words of wisdom.

"This is exactly how people get killed," I said under my breath.

Before I can turn back into the hallway, the door swings open. I now have no choice but to look inside. I see nothing but a small kitchen. Outdated and seems to be out of place in such a nice hotel. It's old and rustic, like it belongs in a vintage suburban home. There's a man sitting at the edge of a wooden dining table. I notice he's slumped over and seems to be out of it. The feeling of depression fills the room as I see he's drinking whiskey straight from the bottle. *Anyone who doesn't even have the will to drink from a glass is someone who needs help.* So I take one step inside, wanting to say something. Within a blink, he moves quickly and grabs a gun off the table. Before I notice, he places it below his chin and lets out a loud yell.

"AAAAAHHHHHHHHHHH!" he screamed as if he was gathering the strength to pull the trigger. I turn my head away from the sight with urgency and hear it. *BANG.* The sound of rain filled the room as I closed my eyes and tried to step back into the hallway. I sprint away to the next room across the hall, terrified of what I just witnessed, hiding from the truth.

I break through the *fourth* door just trying to get away and see a man, maybe in his early 30s. Instantly I am shaken with a thick vibe of creativity and innocence. I feel so much peace and comfort from this place that I completely forget about the last room. It's only a tiny bedroom, and the décor is simple with just a bed and tv being the focal points. The man is sitting in the corner working on some kind of project, typing away at his laptop on a simple dinner tray. He tilts his eyes just slightly enough to see me without moving away from his task. He acts as if he was expecting me to be there but was focused on something more important. He moves with haste to finish before the morning but with so much care and passion. *I must know why,*

Completely drawn in by my curiosity, I move around to see his *screen*. He doesn't miss a keystroke as I step forward, like a small fawn looking for food, deeper into the room. I finally see the screen as he hits the "ENTER" button. He stops and moves back into his seat with a sigh of joy.

"This is great!" He said, thinking out loud. Obviously overjoyed with his work, he reaches over and grabs his drink like a reward. It's a whiskey neat. Just whiskey poured in a small glass, nothing special. The poor man's cocktail, but such a sophisticated drink, if the right liquor. I only know this because it's my mom's drink of choice. Whiskey can make people angry and do stupid things. But the man reveled in it. Found creativity and passion in every glass.

"Hi Jack." He said, placing the glass back down on his makeshift desk.

"This is very unexpected today, honestly. But I have to say; I'm incredibly happy you made it." He continued, making me feel awkward as he turned the laptop to face me.

He's writing something, an essay or a story. I read the first and second lines with enthusiasm until I start to read the third line.

"The man is sitting in the corner working on some kind of project. Typing away at his laptop on a simple dinner tray."

I am thrown through the back of my head with déjà vu as I continue to read the last few lines of what he has typed.

"He's writing something, some kind of essay or story. I read the first and second lines with enthusiasm until I start to read the third line."

Time begins to slow as I look up into his eyes, confused. Wondering who he was and how he could be writing precisely what is happening to me, he begins to speak.

"It's time for you to go Jack." He said, now turned around in his chair, glancing at me like I was his flesh and blood.

I get the weird sensation of being controlled by his words and step out of the room. Not sure of what is going on or how I am moving, but something feels right. Like I have always felt this way.

As the door shuts behind me, my body begins to buzz again. Any energy I may have left, drains as I collapse onto the hallway floor. The only question I have as my vision fades and memory goes blank is,

"Why?"

"Where the hell did he go? I'm not mapping his signature anywhere sir!"

"Reload him and continue."

"He is already in the system without a wipe."

"What!"

RETRY? Y/N

"Jack."

A familiar whisper in my ear as I hit the ground hard and hear an eruption of laughter.

I open my eyes and see nothing but bright fluorescent lights above me. A hand reaches out and grabs ahold of mine. It's *Molly,* and she seems to be embarrassed as she speaks again.

"I didn't even hit you that hard Jack" she whispered.

"Ok, come on guys. Like I said, no messing around. This is a test, and I don't want to have to fail you because of this." Mr. Cook said as he looked up from his work.

I stand straight up with a chill down my spine. Burst

images of the girl I loved being lit like a bonfire blister into my mind. I reach up to wipe my eyes, trying to understand that it was all just another dream. *But it can't be.* I thought, still feeling her warm blood drip down my face. I pull my hands down from my face and see Mr. Cook staring at me with a confused look on his face.

"Ook... Jack, can you please take a seat? The rest of the class is trying to pass this test." Mr. Cook said with frustration in his tone.

Realizing I'm making a fool of myself, I quickly shake off the dream and sit down. As I get comfortable back in my seat, I can feel Molly's eyes on me. I do my best not to engage, but she is persistent. Burning a hole in me with her gaze. The feeling is unbearably uncomfortable, slowly remembering what she did to me in my dream. I look up at the clock and see that I still have another 43 minutes until I'm out of here.

As I try to think of anything other than my dream, I find my #2 pencil waiting for me in the doorway. It brings me joy and a slight chuckle, remembering my anxiety dance was just a few minutes ago. Everything seemed ok until I saw a small piece of paper slide across the desk. It reads,

"Do you know the answer to the first question?"

Completely stunned by the note, I remember pieces of memories from my dream. Being sent to the principal's office that pulled me deep into a spiral of despair. With a reflex, my hand shoots up like a lightning strike.

"Mr. Cook! Can I please go to the bathroom?" I blurted out, trying desperately to escape the moment.

He looked up from his computer, peering at me from above his glasses. Without a word, he gestures with a wave towards the door. I stand up and grab my backpack in a rush, noticing the disapproval of my desk partner. I have no question that I am making the right decision as I make my way out of the class, kicking my pencil in the process. I enter the hallway and feel a wave of relief, realizing I might have dodged a future bullet. *Maybe my dream was a sign I needed to pay attention to.* I thought as the door closed behind me.

The hallway is empty and silent. *I've never seen it like this before.* I thought as I started walking to the bathroom. And I was right. I would never usually leave class. I was always so focused on graduating to escape this city and hopefully start somewhere fresh. *But why does this moment feel so familiar? This is about the same time I walked to the office in my dream. How is this possible?* I questioned myself, hoping I was somehow wrong.

I hear commotion as I open the door to the boy's restroom. With my mind more concerned about my dream, I step inside. I find two guys wrestling on the bathroom floor, screaming at each other. One seems to want nothing to do with the situation, begging to be let go.

"Get off me man! I paid you the money I owed yesterday!" one said, doing his best to fight off his assailant.

"Not good enough kid. You're going to learn how to

show some respect." Demanded the guy on top, landing blow after blow on the other.

I stop dead in my tracks when I catch a small glimpse of the bully's face. He was my bully as well. My older brother. Only here to sell drugs or collect debts he was owed. I always wondered why he would give out drugs on credit. But as I watched him pummel the kid under him, I realized this was why. He enjoyed beating the ones who couldn't pay him on time. Even when they did, he would always disapprove like he was waiting for a reason to strike with violence. *Of course I would walk into this.* I thought as he stopped to catch his breath and begins to notice that he was no longer alone. His head starts to tilt up in my direction like he can smell me. Smell my fear. I feel as if time stops around me, giving me a second to make a swift decision. *Do I turn and run? Or do I stand my ground?*

"What. The fuck. Are you doing here Jack?" Kyle said.

I can feel the sweat peel out of my pores as I tell myself to say something. *Can I still run?* I ask myself but hear a loud reply from the depths of my consciousness. *"NO!"*

"Get lost Jack, or you get two beatings today," Kyle said, promising me more than my usual.

I begin to make my way for the door when I hear a soft female voice enter my mind.

"Never settle for second best. Always fight for what is right. And never forget who loves you."

It stops me without a second thought. It was the sister on my favorite TV show, Jackie. A character I looked up to when it came to morals and doing the right thing. I feel that I've received most of my moral compass from her. She would always stand up to bullies and help those who needed it. A savor. So with her in mind, I close my eyes, take a deep breath, and turn back around.

"Stop Kyle!" I demanded with a nervous energy in my voice.

Unconvinced and annoyed that I would even think about stepping in the way of this, Kyle stops and stands up.

"What do you think you're gonna do Jack? Beat me up if I don't?" he said, laughing with irritation in his tone.

The kid sees his opportunity and sprints to escape, knocking me into the stall doors.

"Now look what you did Jack. Do you think I'm just gonna let this one go?" Kyle stated, wiping the blood off his knuckles.

"You can't go around beating people up Kyle. It's not right." I said, regretting my decision of leaving class.

"Oh, is that right?" He sarcastically asked, stepping closer in front of me. "Well, I'll tell you what. For now on, each time someone owes me money, or I just don't like the way they look, I'll make sure to save all my energy and anger for when I get home. Just. For. You." Kyle said with determination in his eyes. Giving me a very weird feeling in my chest making my blood boil with an anger.

My whole body surges to cut him in half with a frustration of ignorance. A feeling that is unlike me but seems like home.

"And we're gonna start right now." Kyle said cracking his knuckles, stopping in striking distance.

Kyle begins to lunge forward as I feel the moment slow again. This time is different though. Seconds turn to minutes as my mind races, thinking of my next move. Thoughts of escaping or fighting back flood my brain but I am out of time. Then, a unique thought crosses my mind. *What if I could just stop time?* I asked myself, getting a feeling of some sort of barrier holding me back. As my mind attracts to the idea, I mentally push with everything I have, watching his fist get closer to contact. I fall into a weird state of mind in the split of a second as Kyle freezes. Minutes become hours and my mind calms. *How is this possible?* I thought, regaining control of my body and letting out a deep breath. I step to the side, staring at Kyle's fist like a statue at a museum. Studying the inconceivable, my mind melts and drips into my stomach, telling me that what I am seeing isn't real. The longer I have my eyes open, the more I question my own sanity. I begin to speak out loud, talking to myself.

"Am I dreaming again?" I said, listening to my voice echo in the silence.

I begin to take steps back, trying to understand the moment when I hear a sound come from outside the door. *BUZZZ*

I look behind me and I can hear sounds of the school

start to increase in volume. Before I can take a second to turn back, I hear Kyle's voice.

"Catch." Kyle said, throwing something with an evil grin on his face.

I catch what seems to be a large bag filled with mush-rooms as the door swings open. It's the school security guard and he locks his eyes on me as he steps into the bathroom.

"Oh, what do we have here?" he said, grabbing the bag from my hands. "A big o' bag of magic mushrooms ay?" he continued, inspecting the bag, knowing damn well what he was looking at. I am in awe with the current events and I continue to play along trying to understand.

"It's not what it looks like, man. Those aren't mine." I said, trying to convince the guard of the truth.

"It never is, MAN." He said, mocking my tone. "They're my best friends, sisters, cousins, boyfriend, right?"

"They aren't mine! They are his!" I shouted, pointing behind him, watching Kyle move out of the bathroom.

"Honestly, I've seen better actors in this school. Who's are they then kid? You're the only one in here." He stated with a high level of mockery. Just over his shoul-der, I watch my brother exit the room, Still with that smile on his face. Annoyed by the guard's attitude, and still trying to understand the last few moments, I take a deep breath. I try to recenter myself, slowly putting the pieces together while the guard motioned towards the door and demanded.

"You're comin' with me kid."

With the dread and anger filling my eyes, I step towards the door, knowing this would happen.

One way or another.

CHAPTER

X

LOADING...

_____

At this point, I'm not surprised that I've ended up in the principal's office once again. There aren't too many things that would surprise me now. I've witnessed the unimaginable. I wish I could tell someone but who would believe me. I would be just another crazy person in the alley.

"The alley!" I think out loud in the middle of Principle Collin's lecture.

My mind hones in and remembers my dream—the alley where I first met the girl in the hood. I don't even take a second to continue to listen to Mr. Collins and head straight for the door.

"Mr. Aleister! I am not finished with you!" he screamed as the door slammed behind me.

I continue to sprint out of the campus with the determination to find her. It takes only a few minutes until I wrap the corner of my work and see the alley. I slow to a walking pace, looking for anything or anyone who might resemble her. Even the smell of a cigarette would give me more to work with. I scour every inch of the streets in just under an hour but find nothing. I even asked a few people if they had seen her, but no signs of her. I almost give up hope until I try to retrace my steps from that night.

"Maybe I'll try the house with the basement," I said to myself, still running but feeling I've exhausted everything I had. The more I remember the dream, the more my mind forgets. It's almost as if I'm not supposed to remember. Like a piece of my mind is being deleted. I struggle to put every ounce of energy I had to continue, knowing exactly where the house was.

I make it to the house, and I'm greeted by something that completely shifts my mind's attention. A 1967 *Mustang* parked in the driveway. I am stunned by its beauty. Deep black paint and chrome accents. It gives me a yearning to drive it but do my best not to let it distract me from my mission and head straight for the door of the house.

Should I knock? I thought to myself, second-guessing my plan. *Are you just going to walk into someone's basement?* Feeling afraid but determined, I grab ahold of the handle and push the door open. I only get a small glimpse inside before I feel a forceful hit to the back of my head, knocking me unconscious.

"Sir, I'm still not receiving his signature. He continues to be misled by this woman. I thought it would help the extraction process."

"No matter. He will never leave this place. Prepare the Paradise program."

BRAIN DAMAGE

When I wake, I just lay there like a hangover just hit me like a truck. Feeling the cold, wet concrete on my face. The smell of dust fills the air, but I get the sense something is missing. *Cigarette smoke.* I remember this moment as I open my eyes and find myself back in the basement, tied to the post. With everything I've gone through to get here, I am still anxious about what is going on. Hoping that it was her that brought me here. I sit up and notice I don't have chains around my ankle. Instead, I have rope. Just as tight as last time.

"This is different," I said out loud, hoping the outcome of this wasn't.

"Hi. Jack." A deep voice called out from the corner.

Knowing who it was, I begin to panic, figuring that I've made a mistake in rescuing the hooded girl. That all was lost. That I failed.

"Do you really think you could just find her earlier in the day and I wouldn't notice?" He continued, approaching me from within the dark.

"This always has to happen Jack. Don't you know that already?" he stated.

Slowly forgetting my dream more and more as time goes by, I question myself. *I hardly recognize his face, but he seems familiar*, I thought. Within just seconds, my memory slips and I start to cry with fear of why I was there. I couldn't even remember how I got into this situation.

"You see Jack, this place is something of a work of art. A masterpiece per se. It may have its small imperfections, but it will always correct itself." The man explained as I continued to struggle, now screaming for help. I close my eyes as I watch him pull a chrome pistol from his side and put it to my head. *This can't be it. This can't be the end.* I repeated in my head, waiting to hear the blast of my fate being sealed. Feeling the cold sweat of death approaching, I find peace as a small female voice speaks to me. *BANG!*

"Wake up Jack."

BUZZZ

"Getting rid of his recent memories will help, but I'm still having trouble containing him."

"Leave that to me. He's due for a checkup."

SPEAK TO ME

"I've always been mad, I know I've been mad, like the rest of us...
Very hard to explain why you're mad, even if you're not mad."
-Pink Floyd

I find myself inside of a small dark room with no windows. The room is a perfect square with me on a single bed in the center. I can see a steel door across from me, surrounded by painted white cinder block walls. I lay there for only a few seconds, staring at the door when the light above me turns on. A wave of anxiousness and panic flows through my body. I try to get out of the bed, but I can't move. I look down at my arms and legs to find restraints tying me down the bed frame. My body swells with sweat as the door makes a familiar buzzing sound.

BUZZZZZ

The door opens and a man steps inside. He's pushing a wheelchair with a clipboard in his other hand. As he closes the door, I notice that he is a tall, lanky man. He is wearing a dingy white doctor's coat, stained with coffee and ink from his pens in the chest pocket. Still unable to budge, I feel the air become thin and crisp, watching him walk up to the side of my bed.

"Good morning Jack. How did we sleep?" The man asked with his voice muffled by his face mask. I can sense he is smiling from the tone of his question, but it makes me feel uneasy. *This doesn't feel right,* I thought, while he looked into my eyes with a piercing stare.

"Not going to answer me today?" he said with doubt in mind and tilting his head with frustration.

"Well, we remember what happens when you don't talk to me right Jack?" He asked, whipping his body back and slamming his hands down onto my restraints.

I flinch back from the force, feeling the heat of his breath and the fire from his energy. It's as if I can see the darkness flowing from his coat. His eyes grow wide and curl as he lifts the sleeve of my shirt, exposing my forearm. I look down to see my skin is serrated with old cuts and scabs in every direction. I can feel my sweat soak my shirt as I watch him slowly dig into his coat pocket. He pulls out a small knife as if it were being presented to me, like a gift. I tremble with fear when I see the shine of the blade, knowing what might come next.

"HEL-" I begin to cry out for help but am quickly snuffed out by his palm. His aura grows darker as he becomes impatient, gripping the knife tight.

"Now now mister. No one's gonna hear you." He whispered as if he was now having fun.

"And you really think someone is going to believe you?" He continued, letting out a daunting giggle. "So, are you going to answer me, special little Jack?"

I blink profusely, gasping for air as he pulls his hand from my mouth, running the knife against the 1000 scars on my arm. I let out an uneasy and terrified reply.

"Yes. I slept great." I said, shivering with fear of what comes next. He quickly stands up and leans back, still looking down at me, waiting for more.

"And then you ask?" he quickly asked with hope and excitement.

I lay there stunned and confused by the question, watching him slightly sway back and forth. His tone shifts to a deep and demanding voice, whipping his body back down to the edge of my bed with fierce power.

"ASK MEE!!" he yelled.

"ASK ME, ask me! ask me, askmE!" he repeated faster and faster, changing the tones of his voice each time he presented the answer. Pulling down his mask, he lets out a final deep demand.

"ASK! ME!"

I feel the spit of his question as he reveals his face

for me to see the devilish grin. His smile is sharp and yellow, with saliva drooling from his gums. His face is young and innocent looking but is twisted with an evil intent. The iris of his eyes shrink to the size of a needle as I begin to answer his question.

"How did you sleep?" I asked cautiously, awaiting another mood swing.

"I slept amazing! THANK YOU for asking!" He replied, acting as nothing had just happened.

His answer brings a slight feeling of relief as he begins to relax. He stands back up and places the small knife back into his coat pocket. I start to contemplate any possible way of being free of this room when I notice a syringe placed on the seat of the wheelchair. He sees my eyes lock onto the needle and lets out a chuckle, reaching down to grab it. He picks up the syringe and motions to it with his other hand.

"Oh this?" he said while displaying his grin again, showcasing the needle as it squirts into the air. "I remember you don't like this part Jack."

I shake my legs and pull my arms in a final chance to break through my restraints, but it's no use. I can feel the sweat puddled on my chest as I squirm to be away from here. My bondage becomes tighter with every movement I make, forcing me to submit. My body slows with exhaustion from resisting my fate as he leans down slowly.

"I love this part." He whispered, placing the tip of the needle to the right side of my head.

My eyes roll back as I feel the needle puncture my temple and enter my brain. The pain is insufferable but somehow familiar as I grow hazy and tired. I feel my body begin to doze off as I hear him continue.

"After all, it's Tuesday!"

"He still has no recollection."

"Good. Let's hope it stays that way. Also, get rid of his follower. We can't have another mistake."

CHAPTER

XIII

PARADISE

TUESDAY 7:06 AM

"Good morning Jack! How did we sleep?"

I wake up to the sound of my sister calling out to me. My door opens and I see her standing in the hallway, dressed like she's ready for school. I shuffle to make sure I am dressed, but I realize I'm still wearing the same clothes from the night before.

"Are you riding with me or going with Kyle?" Kim asked as she smiled, happy to see her little brother.

I freeze and stare at her clear skin and wide-open eyes as white as her teeth. Her hair was freshly washed and tied up in a ponytail. She had a simple blue dress that draped past her knees and a glow that seemed to be untouched by this tainted world. It was as if she had never tried drugs. Never got addicted. Happy.

I continued to judge her while she grew impatient.

"Ooook." She said with confusion in her voice and turned away.

Overjoyed with her appearance, I spring out of bed, needing answers. While I get ready, I have this strong feeling that I'm forgetting something. Like there's a piece of me missing, but I continue to gain excitement from what I just witnessed. I grab my backpack and have flashbacks as I reach for my #2 pencil, giving me a feeling of déjà vu.

I make my way into the hallway and almost get run over by my older brother.

"Woah, watch out little man." He said, sliding by me like he was a star quarterback. I watch in awe as he walks by without calling me a name or punching me.

"You rollin' with me today, J?" he asked, heading towards the kitchen.

As I watch him go into the kitchen, I notice that the hallway is different. Perfect white walls with our family pictures hung up every couple of feet. Clean and stain-free carpets complete with a fancy runner down the center. The air was fresh and without the smell of cigarettes. Only the smell of bacon. I feel my heart bounce to the kitchen when I hear my mother call for me.

"Come on Jack. Your food is getting cold." She calmly said, knowing I was awake.

I rush into the doorway to find my brother and sister sitting there at the table. They were having a quick conversation about what was going on with me this morning.

"He was just staring at me like he had never seen me before," Kim said while I stepped in.

"Good morning sweetheart! Go ahead and sit down. Gotta make sure you've got enough energy for the day!" my mother said, spinning around from the stove.

I drop my backpack, completely stunned that Mother acknowledged my presence. It was only just last night that she screamed at me to go to bed so her "friend" wouldn't think I was a worthless bum. And now I'm looking at her in the kitchen, noticing that she's probably been cooking since 5 AM. She had a gray dress with small heels on. Her hair and makeup were done perfectly, probably before everyone woke up, as if she didn't want to be seen without it. Her smile grows while I take a seat at the table, and she returns to the bacon frying on the stovetop. I pick up my fork, and before I take my first bite, I hear footsteps coming down the hallway.

"Good morning everyone!" a deep voice behind me said.

"Mornin' Dad." My brother said with food in his mouth.

I looked up at Kyle, stunned as he spoke. Realizing he just said "dad". As the man passes by me, he pats me on my shoulder. A deep fire is ignited inside me as I see his face smiling down on me. I am instantly reminded of everything he did to me and the rest of the family due to him selling crack out of the "back door" of our apartment. I clench my fork so tight, I feel I would break my hand if I squeeze any tighter. He sits down at the head of the table and looks right up at me, wondering if I am ok.

"Hey Jack. What's going on buddy?" he asked, obviously noticing I was dealing with something internal. He had a look in his eyes of pure concern, a face I've never seen him make before. I begin to awkwardly relax and speak a soft couple of words.

"Oh, um, nothing father," I replied, looking back down at my plate, waiting to be yelled at.

"Father? Haha!" he said, laughing and picking up his cup of coffee. "I don't think I've ever heard you call me that. What happened to Dad?" he said, continuing to chuckle.

My mind flies with every type of explanation of how this is happening but I can't pinpoint the answer. *I thought you were in jail. Am I going mad?* Talking to myself, questioning my sanity. *Something doesn't feel right about this.* As happy as I should be to see my family like this, I only feel more alone knowing what was.

Awkward from the situation, I look over at my watch and it reads,

7:36 AM

"Let's go Jack. I gotta stop at the store." My brother

said, picking up his keys and motioning with his hand. I jump out of my seat with food still in my mouth and rush to get my backpack. Excited to break away from the awkward moment, I head for the front door.

"Don't forget your lunches boys!" my mother shouts.

We get outside to my brothers' car. It's a 1967 *Mustang*, with deep black paint and chrome accents. My dream car.

"Let me just put this in the back," he said, grabbing something from the seat and throwing it into the trunk.

With my mind beginning to be brainwashed with the excitement of this new world, he starts the ignition and I hear the roar of the engine. The sound gives me goosebumps as the car purred, calming to a soft idle. I open the heavy steel door and it lets out a small creek as most old cars do and I sit down on the black leather bench seat. *This car is amazing.* I thought, looking at the polished wood inlays and dark walnut steering wheel.

"Seat belt little bro," he said, revving the gas and putting the car into first gear. I quickly buckled up and watch my apartment fade out of sight as we pulled away.

What's going on? I thought to myself, *why is everyone so friendly and perfect?*

We begin to pick up speed and my brother reaches for the radio. The speakers let out a slight sound as he turned it on.

BUZZZ

He seems to be in a great mood, dancing and singing along with the song playing. I think the song title is *Paradise*, but I'm too focused on trying to make sense of it all as we drive by the late bus.

We get to school, and I head straight to my first period within a dazed state. I shake off my thoughts about the previous hour as I get set for the class. I do my best to zone out on the subject, focusing on only what's in the moment. The lesson flies by in the blink of an eye and it seems my day is off to a great start. I head out into the hallway with a smile on my face after the teacher dismisses the class. The corridor fills with the kids of my school. Leaning on the newly installed lockers, waiting for their friends to meet up. Some rushing to their next class, hoping to make it to the other side of the campus. And some taking their time, talking with everyone they know. But everyone was happy. Even the kids running to their next period. They all had smiles on their faces with bright warming auras around them. It was the same feeling I got from Kim this morning. Just full of life and untouched by this cruel world. *But was I mistaken in thinking this world was so cruel?* I thought, contemplating the idea of a world without pain.

"Hey what's up Jack!" a guy said, walking past me, "Looking good bro! I like the fresh jacket." He said, shooting me with his finger guns.

I completely ignore him, feeling I am in some kind of twilight zone, forcing me to look down with an unusual embarrassment. I step into my second period, still looking down at my shoes. I recognize the tile floor as I walk in on autopilot and hear someone shift up in their chair, making the legs squeak against the ground. Before I have a chance to look up, I hear a soft voice.

"Hi Jack!"

Physics 2 on Tuesdays at 8:30 am. My favorite class of the week. The class I had with Molly. I thought as I slowly glance up through my brow as she continues to talk to me, staring into my eyes with excitement.

"Um...so...I'm sorry to bug you with such a basic question, I know you're super busy, but I'm pretty sure there's a test today and I need your help." She said nervously.

I could see her anxiety race as she squirmed in her seat, waiting for my reply. Feeling as if I've been thrown through a brick wall with questions, I gently get pushed aside from behind.

"Standing there like a deer in the headlights isn't gonna pay the bills kid. Coming through," Mr. Cook said as the rest of the class followed him, all of them cheerful and happy to be there.

Stricken with even more *déjà vu* and still hazy from this morning, I make my way to my seat and sit down next to Molly. She is still looking at me, gazing at me. I can feel her eyes undressing me as if she were daydreaming about kissing me. I can't help but sweat in confusion as Mr. Cook stands up from his desk and begins to address the class.

"Good morning class!" he said while I pulled out everything I needed from my backpack.

"Today is an easy day!" Mr. Cook started to say, and I continued to recite the rest of his statement in my head. *Filled with fun and laughter and... a pop quiz!"*

"Filled with fun and laughter and... a pop quiz!"

The class lights up with small cheers as if they were all waiting for this. Excited to exercise the knowledge they have gained. But I couldn't get over the fact that I knew exactly what was to happen next. Like I have lived this moment before.

"Jack," Molly whispers, still waiting to ask her question. I sit straight up in my seat and notice the clock hanging on the wall.

8:33 AM

"What the fuck is going on?" I said under my breath as Mr. Cook began to hand out the test.

I look down at the first question of the quiz, but I already know what it reads.

"What does EMC squared stand for?"

My mind rushes in every direction possible as I start to realize familiarities of this moment. *Why do I get the feeling I've done all this before? And it feels like more than once.* I asked myself, darting my eyes back and forth through the room, feeling my heart beat faster and faster. Searching for some possible explanation.

I feel a soft touch to the back of my elbow as Molly attempts to gain my attention. Completely surprised, I thrust my arm forward with a tickle of chills.

"And there will be no 'lovey-dovey' time during this test," Mr. Cook said as the class softly chuckles, turning Molly a bright red with embarrassment.

This has definitely happened, I thought, looking into the doorway and remembering when my #2 pencil was mocking me. *Almost word for word has been said, but everything is slightly different.* I thought, pulling my #2 pencil out of my backpack.

The right side of my head starts to ache, building in pain as I stare at the pencil, trying to remember anything. A note slides across my desk from Molly and it reads.

"Do you know the answer to the first question?" My mind flashes to a memory of me getting caught cheating and her breaking my heart in front of the class. How she made me feel worthless and unlovable by anyone in this world. How I was suspended because of it. How I lost my job because of her and the video online making me a "famous creep". How I felt that night. I completely drowned in emotions and the urning to die, to be free of the world beating me down each day. Then a thought hits me, halting my reflections of pain.

The girl in the hood.

With overwhelming alertness, I perk up. Feeling every hair stand up on my body from remembering the girl from the alley. The one who smelled of *jasmine*. Her deep blue eyes become the only thing I can see. My mind becomes flooded with memories of a past life. A dream. *Maybe it's more than just a dream?* I ask myself.

It all happens so fast that my headache becomes too much to handle. My vision begins to blur, but it all stops with a simple thought. *If everything is the same, if I am reliving this day, then she is somewhere out there. Alive!* I thought, clinching my chair as if I would fall off. I get a surge of energy and shoot up from the desk. Mr. Cook quickly looks up and watches me grab my backpack as I start to move for the door.

"Where do you think you're going?" he said.

I don't even give him a second to wait for my response as I push the door open, basically swinging it off the hinges. I picture the bridge where I last saw her and begin to sprint down the school's halls. Feeling as if I need to run faster with confidence in every step building, that I will find her. I fly out into the courtyard with a need for answers. I run as hard as I can, not caring if my lungs can take the beating. I don't stop until close enough to see the hill just before the bridge. *She has to be there. I have to know what is happening.* I thought, slowing to a walking pace. As I look down at my watch, I feel the bridge in sight.

As I slow to a stop in front of the underpass, I notice I am alone. It's just the way it was the first time I was here. Same wooden bench off to the side, same overflowing trash can, and the same amount of leaves scattered across the cobblestones. *Of course she wouldn't be here, I'm too early. But she will be here. I can feel it.* I thought, walking over to the bench. I sit down and reassure myself that I will see her again. That she is alive.

I sit there and wait for hours with undying motivation to understand what this all means, but I grow fatigued from the sun and watching the time tick past. Repeating to myself words of motivation to keep me away from falling asleep.

I'm not moving from this bench until I see her. She will be here. I just know it.

THE GIRL IN THE HOODED JACKET

11:11 PM

"Are we having fun yet?"

I wake up to the sound of a female's voice and the darkness of the night. My eyes open wide when I realize I dozed off and look around the area to see no one. I feel chills across my neck as if someone is behind me. Watching me. Waiting for something. A cold breeze sweeps the leaves as I hear a breath in my ear.

"Make a wish." The voice whispers again, making me jump off the bench like a scared animal. Shaken with fear, I begin to panic, believing there is someone with me. Asking me the same question as the girl in the hood. Still looking for some reasoning behind it all, I hear the sound of footsteps as the wind dies. I notice someone walking down the hill towards the bridge. The closer they get, the more I realize that it's a girl. She's wearing boots, dark jeans, and a long jacket with the hood up.

It's her! I scream to myself, overjoyed that she was alive. I stand there in an awakened state of consciousness, knowing I was right in thinking she would be here. And there she was. I couldn't see her face, but I was sure it was her. I begin to feel my body pulsing to run up to her and squeeze, but I am quick to stop my flow of emotions. The uneasy feeling of this new life of mine makes me cautious. I take a step towards her, crunching down on the leaves beneath my feet, hoping I was correct. As she gets closer, my heart pounds harder. I make a final step into the middle of the walkway, cutting off her path. She stops and looks at me through the top of her hood. I can feel her eyes questioning why I was there while pulling down her hood and letting out her long black hair. I melt as I look into her blue eyes once again, seeing her standing there in front of me. Alive.

"Hi there." She said, "Do you mind if I get by?" Motioning behind me through the underpass.

Does she not remember me? I thought, feeling my heart stop and drop to the ground. *I thought she would know who I was, like last time. I thought she was my future wife.* I grow pale white as I question my sanity and move to the side to open her path. Even though every-thing in my life is now full of love, I get the feeling of wanting to die all over again as she passes. My throat is tight and dry as I do my best to speak. *SAY SOMETHING!* My mind calls out, forcing me to focus. I think of only one question I wanted to know.

"What's your name?" I asked.

She suddenly stops just before the bridge and turns around. Looking at me from head to toe, wondering if I should get a response from her. Staring at me as if I somehow knew her and she didn't recognize me.

"My name is Jack," I said, extending my hand, des-perately wanting to know who she was.

She smiled and placed her hands behind her back as if she were ready to take a bow.

"Lucy." She replied. "Nice to meet you Jack."

The wind picked up and the leaves blew across our path, making learning her name extra special. But for some reason, I always knew that.

We stand there, looking at each other, wondering if the other is going to say something. The moment alone was good enough for me. Just to see her. Before she has a chance to turn back around and continue walking, I hear *footsteps*. Growing in speed behind me.

"NO! This cannot be happening! This cannot happen again." I scream out in a panic as I feel the sudden rush of wind pass me by.

"Run Jack!" said a shadowed figure wielding a katana.

"STOP!" I yelled as hard as I could, hoping to get his attention, knowing exactly who he was.

Lucy looks up at the man and loses her smile. She has the look of absolute terror. Before she can beg, he leaps, thrusting the blade forward. The moment feels like it freezes in time as he winds up to deliver the death blow. I jolt forward, reaching out for her but it becomes too late as I watch the blade pierce through her chest, inch by inch. She cries out in pain and begs for help. I take one last step and throw myself into the man as he pulls the blade out of Lucy's heart.

"What the fuck kid? You have to run!" he screamed after getting tackled and dropping the sword.

I spring back up and rush to my knees at Lucy's side. I try to focus on how to save her and what I need to do to stop the bleeding, but the blood won't stop. It just keeps pouring out of her. I apply pressure to the wound, but it squirts like a cracked damn about to crumble. She lets out a soft cry to have me stop, but I must try. *I can't lose her again.* I refocus on the wound and fall into her eyes, now teared and drained.

"You're going to be ok! I'm here Lucy! You're going to be ok." I cried.

I see her mouth move, but she doesn't make a sound. *"Jack."*

I feel her life slip away in my arms as she becomes cold and lifeless. I scream out like a wolf crying for the moon. *How could I let this happen again! I should have remembered. I was the only one in this world that knew this would happen. I should have known!* I thought to myself, crying onto her blood-soaked jacket.

I sit there, holding her, for only a few moments before I hear the sound of metal scraping the stones of the pathway.

"I told you to run kid," he said, standing behind me. "Now we have to do this the hard way."

As the words came out of his mouth, I realized that he also knew the past lives I lived.

"You are just so damn fucking persistent. Don't you get it already?" he continued.

"Why do we have to kill her? I don't understand what this has to do with her." I said, laying Lucy's body softly on the ground. Still facing her, he replies with a question within his answer.

"Do you really think this has anything to do with Lucy?" he asked.

Before I can comprehend the question, the point of his blade touches my back. Taking in a deep breath, I know what is to happen next. I feel the sword enter my skin and into my spine. As the edges slowly cut through my muscles like water, I have no pain, no emotion. Only acceptance. I look down to see the blade exit my chest. A quick thrust followed by a gradual gush of red onto

Lucy's body. I feel free as he pulls the katana and I fall onto Lucy. My mind goes black as I hear him speak.

"Let's try this again from the beginning."

I feel myself lifted out of my body as I did before but at a slower pace. My vision opens and I can still see the bridge with the cobblestone path like a witness to a crime scene. I watch the older me dump the same 5-gallon gas can over our bodies and reach into his pocket. He pulls out a silver zippo lighter with the #85 engraved into its side and sparks the flame.

Wait, is that the same lighter I was given? I thought, reaching down into my right pocket and pulling it out. *The silver zippo with the Roman numerals engraved on the side.* As his lighter falls at my body's feet, the flame ignites the gasoline.

I don't understand. What do I have to do? Why has this happened more than once? I continued to contemplate the difference between a dream and reality. As I try to understand, I lift higher and higher, watching the flames rise in height. My mind is mentally drained and working on fumes, but I have a burst of energy as the heartache becomes rage. Engulfed with anger and confusion, feeling myself building up for something next. It starts with hearing a small buzzing sound until it grows to become loud as a train's horn. My vision is burned with a blinding white flash as the sound is too much to bear.

"Sir! I don't understand. He's breaking through the barrier!"

"Fix it! Now! He will corrupt the system if he reboots!"

CHAPTER

XV

P4RAD1SE

TU3SDAY 6:66 AM

"Good morning Jack! How did we sleep?"

I wake up to the sound of my sister calling out to me as my alarm goes off. *BUZZZ*

My door opens and I see her standing in the hallway. I jump out of my bed like it was on fire, feeling a constant flow of *déjà vu*, turning my brain to a mush of pain. A blast of emotion splits my mind as I look down at my hands, grabbing at my shirt. Feeling the dampness of blood. *Lucy's blood.* I feel a wound where the katana pierced through my chest and remember everything.

My horrible family life turned happy, my social life becoming popular, and Lucy's murder. For some reason, it feels like I have seen it a thousand times now and can't do anything about it. My eyes twitch with vengence as I look up to my sister still standing there.

"Are you riding with me or- "

"Stop!" I demanded, holding out my hand, thoroughly annoyed.

She stood there with a look on her face of disapproval as I began to walk towards her. I try to move past her, gently pushing on her ribs, gesturing to let me through, but I'm stunned to find that she feels cemented to the ground. I look into her eyes as she begins to pucker her lips to speak once again.

"Are you riding with me or with Jacob?" she asked.

I look up in disarray, watching her go through the motions of this day, still trying to complete her part. She looks me dead in the eyes and repeats what I've already heard.

"Ooook." She said with confusion in her voice.

I grow an uneasiness as I feel her body grow light in an instant as she begins to step away down the hall. *Why did she continue, even when I stopped her?* I thought to myself, waiting for my brother to come down the hall. I close the door and take a few steps back into my room as I feel him coming down the hall. I can hear him talk to me through my door as he passes my room.

"Woah, watch out little man." He said as he did before, but I wasn't there. I was still in my room.

"You rollin' with me today J?" he said, as his voice became muffled from the distance of his question.

There was definitely something weird going on, but I couldn't quite wrap my mind around it. I got a sense of chills as I remembered exactly what had happened the last time.

"Come on Jack. Your food is getting cold."

I grow hesitant about what is really going on when I hear my mother greet me as if I just walked into the kitchen.

"Good morning sweetheart! Go ahead and sit down. Gotta make sure you've got enough energy for the day!" Mother said.

A slight hum of pain begins to swell in my head as I wait in my room for the next coming prepared moments. I open my door as I hear my father's footsteps coming down the hallway. Keeping my eyes on him as he greeted my family in the kitchen.

"Good morning everyone."

"Mornin' Dad." Kyle replied, just as I thought he would.

Then I saw it. I watched as my father passed my chair and pat me on the shoulder as if I were sitting there.

With a skeptical cautiousness, I step out of my room in pure investigative mode. I head down the hallway to the kitchen, watching my father continue the conversation with a ghost of me.

"Hey Jack. What's going on buddy?" He asked, talking to an empty seat.

The closer I get, the more my head aches with incredible pain.

"Father? Haha!" he said, laughing and picking up his cup of coffee. "I don't think I've ever heard you call me that. What happened to Dad?"

My entire body tingled with a fear I did not know yet. It was a feeling of regret, knowing the truth. But it all became clear why I was reliving this day and every other time that felt like a dream.

It never was a dream.

The more my mind tried to make sense of it, the angrier I got. *I can't waste my time on this. I must find Lucy before that bastard does.* I thought, now feeling the rage I have built up over the multiple times I've watched her die. I pick up my stuff and grab my brother's keys.

"Let's go Jack. I gotta stop at the store." Kyle said, reaching for the keys I now had in my hand. I hear my mother one last time as I head for the door with determination and fire in my eyes.

"Don't forget your lunches boys!"

D4RK HOR5E

I break through the front door and down the porch steps in an anger-driven sprint. I feel myself growing into an untamable fire, untouchable from being extinguished. I stop and take in the moment of being out of there, looking down on my brother's 1967 mustang. She was calling out for me like a lost lover. As I move around the front of the car and make my way to the door, I get the feeling of Lucy's touch. A drowning of senses. It only fuels my fire. *She is my fire.* Images of Lucy strike my mind with everything she could be. Every movement she would make, every time she smiled, and the sound of her laugh. They filled my thoughts like lost memories.

I feel it chill my bones like a wave of the ocean crossing my chest.

Starting the muscle car, I hear the roar of the engine, continuing to fuel my mission. I get ready to put the car in gear as my brother walked down the steps, talking with an invisible simulation of myself. Just like every time before that. Determined and unwilling to have distraction, I throw the car into first gear, feeling the engine's power, allowing the dark horse to use its maximum potential. I tear into the street with the smoke of the tires and watch the rear-view mirror as my brother tries to open a car door that isn't there. Over and over.

I get the old 67' beauty up to 88 mph on the highway when I notice something wrapped in cloth on the seat next to me. As I reach for it, I hear a loud sound come from the speakers.

BUZZZ

Then only silence. It's a questioning moment, but I continue to be undistracted.

I can feel the wind on my face as I reach to my left and roll my window down, pressing on the gas to go faster. The feeling is something familiar, but never felt this way before. An idea of freedom with work to be done. There is only one thing on my mind. Lucy.

I'm going to kill that Motherfucker.

The faster I drive, the more I feel in control of my decision. I can see an ending to all of this. The deeper I fly through the city, I begin to be slowed by traffic. Stopped cars in the middle of the road. All of them to be accurate. I come to a complete stop behind the blockade when I notice the people on the sidewalk. They are all just standing there. All of them doing some kind of action, frozen in time. I am stunned but not surprised. *How far does this go?* I ask myself, *is this all just a simulation?* I watch the city turn5 on like a switch as I'm c4ught in the middle of the spe3dway. Cars blow past me, shaking the mustang, 2howing me the power of possible impact. I act without hesitat1on. Forcing d0wn the clutch, I give the muscle car the gas she needs and br

SYSTEM SHUTDOWN

"Sir, the system is down!"

"Good. Now reboot the program."

"We really have no idea how the program will react. It could be catastrophic."

"Do it now!"

REBOOTING: PROJECT: 𒅲𒌋𒌋𒁹𒀭𒈨𒌋

Wait *what? How did I get here?* I thought, looking up from my hoodie wrapped up like a ball on my desk. "Physics 2" reads on the chalkboard. *I was just in my brother's car. How am I here? Was it all just a dream?*

TU3SDAY 85:13 AM

I hear the sound of a loud squeak under Mr. Cook's chair which makes me adjust my attention. He looks up from his work and begins to speak.

"Now class, I understand that this has been a hard year. And that being said, I'm willing to forget this test even existed if you answer my one question, Jack?"

I feel the entire class flip around in their seats and look directly at me with dead eyes.

"Why do you do this to yourself?" he continued.

"Why are you always placing yourself in these situations? It's always been your fault that she dies, and you know it." He said as a wave of fear flowed through my blood, causing a shift in my plan.

"You continue over and over to ignore me, but today, Mr. Aleister, you are going to **FEAR** me."

As his final words came out, the entire room felt like it began to shrink and slowly twist. The lights grow dim as my headache vanishes. I can feel my body wanting to run but it is as if I am paralyzed from the idea of the bigger picture. *None of this is real.* Before I get the chance to comprehend an answer, I hear the entire class stand simultaneously.

"Class, we don't want him to get away this time, do we?" Mr. Cook asked.

"No Mr. Cook." They said in sequence.

As I somehow gather my thoughts to finally move my body, I feel the student's hands on me, restraining me to my seat. Each one of them with overpowering strength, restricting me from leaving. I can do nothing but scream out for help. "HEL- "

"Now now mister, no one's gonna hear you." Mr. Cook said like he was now having fun. Instantly, I have a flash of memory. *I heard that before. But where?* I thought, feeling each one of the student's hands like they all wanted a piece.

"So, are you going to answer me, my *special little Jack*?" Mr. Cook continued. I close my eyes and begin to talk myself down from the towering fear of the moment, trying anything to make things clearer. *This isn't real. This isn't real. Snap out of it Jack. THIS ISNT REAL!* I thought, desperately wanting to escape.

"NONE OF THIS IS REAL!" I screamed, opening my eyes and finding nothing but an empty classroom. Stunned that I was correct, I take one moment of relief. Inhaling a deep breath, but it was one moment too long as I witness Mr. Cook materialize in front of me.

"You can't run from me Jack!" he said, now with solid black eyes and pale grey skin. With his tone becoming deeper and more powerful. He begins to shake the walls with merely his voice.

"You will. **DIE** here!"

I quickly jump out of my seat in a hot burst of fear, knowing what would come next if I stayed. I sprint to escape within an instant. As I swing the door open, he lets out a shrieking sound that almost punctures my eardrums. I turn the corner into the hallway looking for for an exit and only get a few steps away until I see the surrounding doors open with force. My eyes grow wide as I watch the students of the school pour out in a matter of seconds. Each one of them like the last. Dead eyes and moving together as one. All of them reaching out to stop me from leaving this hellscape. I do my best to continue through the hallway, but they swarm and engulf me. It becomes harder and harder to push off the hundreds of attempts to restrain me. The closer I get to the front door, the more students lined up to be my demise. *None of this is real. They are all just part of my imagination. This is just a dream. You are the one in control.* I recite to myself on repeat, waiting for the same response from the classroom. But it's no use. I've made it just one step from the outside but am consumed by the overwhelming students surrounding me. I am trapped. It feels like they are all pulling on my body, trying to tear me apart from every direction. And then. I see *her.* She is just outside, leaning on the hood of my brother's car, smoking a cigarette.

A fury of pain and anger flows as my vision becomes dark from the student's bodies covering me head to toe. Feeling the ground on my face as the students continue to pile on, each one of them trying to get a hold of me. This seems to be the end of my story when the burning anger quiets in my mind. It is an emotion of pure bliss and harmony as I forget everything I've ever known about physics and the world around me. Everything I've believed to be accurate and logical. Then a soft but powerful thought comes into my head.

Nothing is impossible.

I feel the thought power me like a lightning rod, fueling my rage and transforming the energy into wrath. My mind becomes clear of any impossibilities, and I feel the weight of the hundreds of students grow light.

"Lucy." I said, opening my eyes and beginning to fight back.

With a blast of emotions, I stand up with ease as the energy around me throws them back with a powerful force. I see her once again as the student's bodies fall beneath me. Stepping through the door, I feel the heat of the day turn into night in a split second. Watching the world around me take a different shape from what I remember. The skies swirled with red and black clouds as if it were the beginning of the apocalypse. But my eyes were set on hers. Stepping closer and closer.

"Took you long enough," Lucy said, stepping out her cigarette and reaching out for my hand. "Shall we take a drive?" she continued, knowing exactly where I intended to go.

"Let's go."

THE BRIDGE

I rip through the city on a vengeful path of saving the girl that now sits next to me. Knowing that everything lies on his death. The release of this madness of continual repeats of a hell I know all too well. *Flying through the empty streets of an apocalyptic town is a great setting for my final stand with this bastard.* I thought, gripping the steering wheel and getting the dark horse up to 111 mph. Without a care in the world about where all the lifeless zombies might be, I push deeper on the pedal. Lucy sits there with a smile on her face, not worried by the gradual gained speed. She reaches down and picks up the item wrapped in cloth and places it between us.

"You're going to need this," Lucy whispered, stroking

the hair away from my face. She unwraps the cloth and I look down to find the exact katana used to kill Lucy the times I failed.

"I won't fail this time," I said, looking back up to the road, determined to end this.

"I know," Lucy replied, now with her hand on my shoulder, powering me to finish this.

"Do you know what you're doing Jack?" She asked, knowing I had no clue.

"I'm going to cut him in half," I replied, allowing my anger to overflow with a twist of my hands on the steering wheel.

"There's something you must know," Lucy said, watching me grow worried from her statement. She begins to explain this place and what is necessary for us to get out. It's a hard pill to swallow but it must be done. As I come over the hill, I see him waiting for me just in front of the bridge. He is surrounded by what I can only describe as an army of civilians of the city. As our eyes connect, he gives me a smirk like he's excited for my arrival. I jump the curb and slide the mustang across the cobblestones, coming to a complete stop. I look over into Lucy's blue eyes and do my best not the drown in them once again as she hands me the katana and speaks.

"Let's go home."

I take a small deep breath and swing the door open. Remembering that nothing is impossible, I step outside and begin to pull the sword from its sheath. The army of people stand there silent. Watching me. Waiting for something. The older version of myself steps in front of them and begins to speak.

"So, you finally figured it out." He condescendingly said. "But I don't think you have what it takes. Prove me wrong Jack."

He then turns around and walks back into the crowd, disappearing within the bodies.

"Kill him." I hear from the back of the group as the countless civilians become vicious in an instant. Each of them baring their teeth, showing me their only weapon to be used. As they begin their charge for me, my stance spreads and I prepare my attack. The more steps they take toward me, the more my head hums. But this time there is no pain. There is only a calming touch. Watching them inch closer, gaining in speed, I remember the confrontation with my brother in the school bathroom. The first five of the mindless zombies leap forward to strike, just a few yards from me. Without moving an inch, I close my eyes and whisper.

"No."

I open my eyes to find the five frozen in time as I intended. With one thought now ringing in my head, keeping my soul from turning black, I strike without mercy. *They aren't real.* I watch as my blade cuts through them with precision and ease, staining the cobblestones with their blood. Dropping all five with one swipe, I see his eyes widen with excitement. Without a second to breathe, I charge the crowd with blood still dripping from the tip and lunge forward. I am fast. Faster than

I could understand but don't lose focus. They all begin their assault, but I fly through them, slicing anything that wasn't air. Cutting my way into them like an overgrown jungle in a hurry. Making a path to victory with blood and carnage in my wake. Even the ones that slip through and attack from behind were met with my edge. Nothing could stop me from my goal.

"You think I've enjoyed this Jack?" I faintly hear over the sounds of steel on bones.

"You think I would do this if I didn't know this was necessary?" He continued, now only a few yards from the splatter of my sword.

"You underestimate this place. Like I said, it will always correct itself."

In a flurry of blood and sweat dripping from my brow, I take one final step forward and lunge the katana deep into the last person in front of him. My eyes grow with fear as I realize the mistake I've made. All I see are deep blue eyes, staring back at me.

"Jack," Lucy muttered through the blood now seeping from her mouth, gripping my blade between her ribs. "It's time to go home now."

Horrified with what I've done, I feel my body tense up but go limp with the pain of my own doing. The one I've been chasing, the one I've held dear throughout this nightmare, killed by my hands.

"You see, Mr. Aleister, the progr4m will always correct itself." I heard as Lucy stumbles back off the blade that sealed her fate. I can do nothing but watch Lucy fall to the ground, reaching out for me with pain in her eyes. I feel hollow. A shell of myself, witnessing the demise of my love.

"You were always supposed to kill her Jack. She has always been the answer." The older version of me spoke, basking in his victory. "She has been the key to our release this entire time. You just needed to figure that out on your own." He continued.

"You're not leaving this place," I said with my eyes beginning to tear. "She told me that this was the outcome. That no matter what I did, I would never be rid of you and this hellish cycle." I continued, letting my truth speak for itself. "I knew it would be hard, but it must happen to finally break free."

He looked up at me with wonder and amazement, questioning his ideas of me. Wondering if he went wrong somewhere in the calculations of my intentions.

"But no. You will not be coming with us," I said, regripping the katana and lunging forward with hatred in my eyes. With one step into the puddles of blood that covered the cobblestone path, my sword plunges deep into the heart of my older self. He has no choice but to take the blow as I follow with a swift right hook to his jaw, knocking him to the ground. As I regain my balance, I watch as he tries to put together words, asking himself. *Why?*

I stand there waiting for some kind of response when I feel the warmth of his blood soaking my shirt as a breeze passes. The chill of this world's touch is a feeling I have missed since the beginning of this walk-through hell.

"You can't live without me Jack," he said, desperately gasping for air. "You will never survive."

There is a wave of passion for this moment, as I feel to be at the end of the road. A cough of blood sprays my face, bringing my attention back to the final death I hope to witness.

"You will be as you were. Just the sad, pathetic little kid you were always supposed to be." He said, using each deep breath to the fullest. With my eyes locked on to his, I stand up to grab the gas can under the bridge, where it always was.

"You will cease to exist without me! Please don't do this!" he said, grabbing ahold of my leg to stop me from finishing this endless cycle. Without sympathy, I kick his hand off with an angry force and pop the cap of the jug of gasoline. *Everything has led to this moment,* I thought, *I can't waste my opportunity.* Tilting the jug to spill, I drench the same clothes I've feared to come from behind in the pungent gas. The smell of blood and gasoline is a mixture I never thought I would sense, but I can feel my mind become victorious as it fills the air.

"You can never erase me," he said, watching me dig into my pocket and pull out my lighter. The one with the #85 engraved on the side of it. *VIIIV.* The same silver zippo that has been in my pocket since the beginning. He reaches out and watches as I take pride in striking the flame, waiting for an answer. I stand there for just a second, coming to terms with the end, looking into Lucy's eyes.

"Do it Jack. Let's go home." She said with an approving smile. With her final breath, she lets out words that light my path.

"I love you Jack."

I watch tears of joy fill Lucy's eyes as I drop the lighter into the stream of gas and ignite the fire of our freedom. Feeling the flames grow higher and the warmth of relief, I softly reply.

"I know. I love you too Lucy."

PERMANENT SHUTDOWN

"I have no idea how he did it, but the entire program is corrupted sir, and I am completely locked out of the system."

"That's impossible."

"Somehow, patient 85 has fought back through the barrier and damaged the data of the system. It doesn't make any sense. I've checked all vitals on both of them throughout the entire project and there haven't been any irregularities."

"Just get us back into the system and ill handle the patients. Guard! Take number 85 to holding."

LUCY

"FEELING numb" is contradictory. This feeling is more of just pins and needles. But I can still feel her blood on my face with the smell of gasoline still in my nose. A sense I will never forget.

With my eyes shut, I feel that I am moving. Slowly rolling. *But will this be any better?* I ask myself, trying to pry my eyes open. I gain enough strength to peak with my left eye as the smell of this new place touches my mind. It reeks of musty metal and damp mold. A scent I recognize but have no memory of. I can hear the sound of my wheels rolling through thick puddles as my eyes open fully and focus. I can see that I am in a long hall-way with a large double door at the end of it. Its décor is of an abandoned hotel with the furniture to go with it. A black and white checkered tile floor and the wallpaper peeling off from its old age. I notice a few openings with bars on the windows and three more rooms on my left.

The hallway seems to get tighter as I continue towards the door, making my growing anxiety, worse. As I roll by the first two openings, I see a person in each room chained to the ceiling. Both gripping the wall between them. They seem to be lip sinking a song of some sort, in sync, without seeing each other. As if they are connected. They stop at the exact time and stare at me as they watch me go by with drone looks of despair.

The closer I get to the next doorway, I can hear a man yelling at the top of their lungs. The sounds shriek in my head as I begin to understand the words screamed.

"KILL ME! DO IT NOW! KILL ME! KILL ME! KILL ME! HAHAHA HA HA HA!"

I have no choice but to look inside and see a man sitting on the edge of his bed, rocking back and forth. With his fingers in his mouth with the shape of a gun, he continues to scream as we lock eye contact.

"PULL IT! PULL THE FUCKING TRIGGERRR!"

I close my eyes away from the sight of someone wanting death so desperately, and they would do anything for the sweet embrace of the unknown. *Anything to get away.* I thought, moving my eyes back down the hallway as my wheelchair stopped at the fourth door. I began to recognize the door as it opened and see a room full of people. As I roll into the large room, I see that everyone is sitting in small groups. Maybe three or four of them to each table. All hunched over with different colored bathrobes and the place smells like a cigar lounge. The person escorting me stops me at a table next to a window and unstraps me from my chair. I notice that four others are sitting next to me, but I pay little attention to them as I am drawn to the trees outside, blowing in the wind. The movement of the branches sparks something inside me that tells me I've made it. That I've made it to the place Lucy described. *Home. But what is this place? Is this what we call home?* I question myself, now looking around at the stained concrete walls and others around me. *Why is there such a negative feeling about this place*? I thought now looking at the people that shared my table.

"Hi Jack. Do you know the answer to the first question?" a girl next to me asked as a #2 pencil rolled in front of me.

"Molly!" I blurted out, knowing exactly who sat next to me. I became shocked to see her face again, but this time she was different. She looked to be at least ten years older than my last confrontation with her in Physics 2. Her hair was up and mangled which seemed to be unwashed in weeks. It was hard to see her like this, but I realized that I may have completed the cycle Lucy spoke about.

With my eyes fixed on Molly's questioning eyes, I feel a chill as I glance over at a man walking up to the table with a plate of food.

"Hey, no lovey-dovey stuff, remember?" the man

stated as I caught a glimpse of his nameplate that read "Cook".

"It was Jack's fault Mr. Cook!" Molly screamed, turning the entire room silent. I feel the eyes of the people around me just as I did in my physics class. *Is this some sort of reenactment of my dreams? Of where I was before?* I thought, turning my head to the window with confusion. *How can I be sure this is real?* I continued to ponder. Before I have a chance to gather my thoughts of this new *beginning*, my nerves fire with fear as I hear a deep voice come from my table.

"I see you're still questioning yourself, Jack." a familiar man said. A voice I thought I would never hear again. I turn around to see his face as he continues to talk to me, but his back is turned to the table.

"I guess your 85th try didn't work out too well, did it?" he said, lighting a cigarette with a silver lighter.

"I told you, it all hinges on her." he continued, letting out a cloud of smoke.

I didn't need to see his face to know exactly who he was. It was the bastard that continually killed the girl I loved. The rage that had dissolved with his death reignited inside me as I began to try to stand up out of impulse.

BUZZZ

"Oh, speak of the devil. Here she comes," he said, motioning towards the door with his cigarette.

All my energy and strength are ripped from my body as I see a hooded girl rolled into the room. I collapse back into my wheelchair as I see her long black hair. I become engulfed in confidence that it's Lucy. I continue to watch as she is pushed to the edge of the room and parked at the far window alone. *That's her. She's here. She was right.* I thought while forgetting to breathe.

"Well? Are you just gonna sit there Jack? Go to your wife." the man said, holding out his pack of cigarettes and the silver lighter.

"You're gonna need these if you don't remember." he continued.

I stand up with the burning desire to see her face again and grab the cigarettes. As I begin to step forward, I can feel my legs are weak like they haven't been used in days. The closer I get to her, the more nervous I feel that I could be wrong. That this hooded girl isn't Lucy.

I stop next to her and gaze out the window. The feeling of worry stops my words from escaping my mouth, but it quickly turns to warmth in my heart as she speaks.

"We made it Jack. Were home." Lucy said, tilting her head and leaning against my arm. "I've missed you, my love."

My heart explodes with love as I feel it flow throughout my body like a river. Her head shifts up towards me as I pull down her hood. *Those blue eyes.* I thought as her face became clear. Memories flooded my mind of happier days before a continuous bad Tuesday. A life filled with love and passion. My thoughts are overwhelmed with a past that I've shared with her. Our first date. Her contagious laugh. Our first apartment. Our wedding day.

Everything that was once forgotten inside that hellish dream returned to me in a flash from just the sight of her skin. Without hesitation, I lean down and kiss her softly, needing the affection. The feeling is blissful, knowing I was reunited with the person I cared the most about. Just as I embrace her lips, the moment turns sour as I hear footsteps from behind me, growing in speed.

"Mr. Aleister!" I heard as the feeling of a blunt object struck my legs, dropping me to the ground. "You never listen do you, my little Jack." a man wearing a mask said, now looking down on me.

With the quick transition of love into hate, I look up to see that it is the doctor that tortured me. Memories of his crooked yellow smile fill my head with a mixture of fear and rage as I hear the man back at my table stand up.

"Leave him alone!" he yelled, balling his hands into fists.

"Oh? So, both Jacks want to test my patience today? It really must be Tuesday after all." the crazy doctor stated, with his attention now set on my old enemy. "Well, your next old man, just after I teach little Jack what happens when he doesn't listen." the doctor continued, still looking up at my rival.

I find my opening and take it with a swift kick to the inside of the doctor's kneecap. I can feel the bone snap under the pressure of my foot as he lets out a cry of agony, bringing him down to my level. Without a second's notice, I see the man who has brought me so much heartache rush to my rescue.

"Run Jack!" he screamed, jumping onto the mad doctor and giving me the time to make my escape.

I quickly shuffle to my feet and grab Lucy by the hand, pulling her up out of her chair. She seems to be fine to stand, but I insist on helping her run. As we bust out of the double doors into the hallway, an alarm sounds along with someone over a loudspeaker.

"Do not let them escape! They are everything to the project! Stop them at all costs!"

Stepping through the thick puddles back down the checkered hallway, I can feel the eyes of the people I passed before. Each one of them exerting energy of joy to see Lucy and I making our escape. Almost as if their own lives depended on it. We continue running through the hallway and into a different corridor that seems to fork off into multiple directions. Every one of them with their own feelings of mystery. Our decision is quickly made when I see three guards wrap the corner on our left and Lucy turns to the right. It feels like I am almost out of strength when Lucy points out a red neon sign that says, EXIT.

It couldn't be that easy, could it? I thought to myself, reaching for the handle to our freedom. I twist the handle only to find it locked with the guards closing in. My mind flares up with an anxiety I know all too well, feeling that I have failed until Lucy hands me the silver lighter.

"The fire alarm." She said, pointing up to the smoke detector above us. I quickly grabbed the lighter hoping this crazy idea would work and light the flame. Using my last ounce of hope, I reach as high as possible to burn the detector. Within just seconds, a different alarm sounds, and I hear the door's lock unhinge as Lucy pushes it open. The sun hits me like a ton of bricks, blinding my vision as we step outside. Lucy is quick to slam the door behind us as we continue our escape. We make it just a few yards outside until I hear the door swing open. I have no choice but to look back only to find the three guards standing there, watching us run. Like they have done all they could. The confusion is overwhelming, but I focus on getting away from this place. We continue to exhaust the little energy we have as we make it over a small hill. I feel my soul pulse when we reach the top and see the bridge. The same bridge that haunts me. I stop dead in my tracks as Lucy begins to try to soothe my thoughts.

"The memories of this place are not real Jack. It was all part of their experiment. Trust me." Lucy said, looking deep into my eyes.

I nodded with the trust she asked for as we continued.

We make our way down the hill and across the cobblestone path up to the bridge, seeing through the other side. We slow to a walking pace as she grips my hand even tighter, knowing the trauma I have built up from this place. I can feel the pain of losing her as we walk into the alleyway under the structure, but the warmth of her hand guides me through.

The feeling of the other side is like I've shed a thousand pounds. The sense of this endless cycle of pain and agony, gone. That I was finally free. That I was finally free to be happy with her.

As a cold breeze hits me along with the newfound happiness of our escape, I feel a slight tickle of pain in my head.

Make a wish.

TO BE C0NT1NUED...

This is the first published story of many from the out-landish mind of **Jack Aleister**. Over the past couple of years, I have studied Jack's history and found countless amounts of evidence proving his existence. Showing that his life was spent searching around the world for artifacts and other rare antiquities with one in particular, the *katana* of King Tutankhamun. He would record his adventures throughout the way, writing detailed descriptions of the different places. Each location with its own *mystical* properties and dangers to be overcome. I recently was able to acquire the few journals Jack was reported carrying. The top of the stack read, *VIIIV*.

Some say the stories of his travels are true. Others say he's due for a *checkup*.

-Christopher Conner

Everything in this book may be wrong.